Atkinson's Absolution

The Reaper Series

Book Six

John Paul Bernett

ATKINSON'S ABSOLUTION

Dedication

I would like to dedicate this entire series to My wife and muse
Beverly Gail Bernett.

ATKINSON'S ABSOLUTION

The Reaper Series

Book One: Atkinson's Administration
Book Two: Atkinson's Armageddon
Book Three: Atkinson's Adversary
Book Four: Atkinson's Apprentice
Book Five: Atkinson's Apocalypse
Book Six: Atkinson's Absolution

Prequels to the Reaper Series

Book One: A Switch in Time
Book Two: A Woman at the Helm
Book Three:...A Date with the Reaper

ATKINSON'S ABSOLUTION

Acknowledgements

My main acknowledgement has to be to my wife and muse, Beverly Gail Bernett; she worked tirelessly to give me the inspiration to write this series of books. She also instilled a belief that I could actually show my work…and for that, I will be forever grateful.

Another massive thanks goes to Gavin Johnson & Lee Coates of V-Edition Media, for their work on all my book covers.

I would also like to credit the skills of the wonderful photographers who have taken my author pictures throughout this series:

Atkinson's Administration	Hunter Tate.
Atkinson's Armageddon	John Orange Photography.
Atkinson's Adversary	Deborah Priestley Photography.
Atkinson's Apprentice.	John Orange Photography.
Atkinson's Apocalypse.	Bita Mills Photography.
Atkinson's Absolution.	Gavin Johnson

I would also like to thank all the people who let me base my characters upon them, and use their photographs to bring them to life; all my characters are, however, purely fictitious.

A round of applause is deserved by my good friend Clare Gollop, who loaned me a computer when mine died during an important stage in the writing of this last book in the series.

Lastly, A big thank you goes out to everyone taking the time to read my words!

ATKINSON'S ABSOLUTION

'And in the End, all that is left is a new Beginning.'

Chapter One

Alice Winters-Chambers' future lay ahead of her, in the brilliant light of the new dawn in the second era of Humankind. The air was sweet...clean and fresh. The sky was the deepest blue that she had ever witnessed. The only sound was the buzzing of the industrious bees, as they gathered pollen from the flowers that grew in abundance all around. Jasmine Lester came up to Alice, and put her arm around her.

As these two lovely ladies who now shared the same colour of skin and accent – unlike when they were within the shelter – Embraced, Jasmin sighed. "All those years of fighting, judgment, and bigotry...because of the colour of my skin. I can't believe it's finaly at an end...but I don't feel any different, I just feel happy."

"This is just the beginning, Jasmine...not being 'caucasian' has had no effect on me whatsoever – in fact, the only people who might object are long dead," said Alice.

"Never to return," agreed Jasmine.

Jasmine rejoined the group of people by the shelter, as Alice looked over the trees and gazed towards the horizon to where the volcano stood. To her surprise, the deadly mountain had been replaced by what looked like one of the ring of purple-topped peaks she'd witnessed when she visited the Realm of Nature, owing to its summit being the same colour. She tried to remember Leeds as it had been with its bustling streets, bars, restaurants, and nightlife – but try as she might, she just couldn't recall those images clearly anymore.

This sensation felt a bit strange to Alice, as only four weeks had passed since she had last stepped out into that once-great metropolis. A calming thought entered her mind as Mother Nature's influence overtook her way of thinking...'*You cannot affect the past this time, Alice – you must put your thoughts towards the new tomorrow.*'

Alice smiled and breathed in the fresh air that was full of the aroma of the forest, taking her first tentative steps away from the shelter.

She could now hear the fast-flowing River Aire. Alice gazed upon the beauty of the morning; the sky was the most vibrant blue her eyes had ever seen – it seemed to emphasize the newness of the day, and indeed, the world. She could hear the buzzing of the bees, but not the sounds of birds, or other animals. Again, Alice delved into the mind of Mother Nature, and received the realization that the animals would not return for a further twelve moons.

Alice felt the arms of Freddie Chambers wrap around her shoulders from behind, as he whispered, "Here is your gift from Mother Nature...you helped make all this possible with your selfless actions."

Alice leaned back, snuggling into Freddie. "I wish I could thank Albert and Doris right now...they are the ones who made all this possible, by all the things they taught me."

"I wonder what became of them..." mused Freddie.

"I am sure they had a wonderful – albeit hard life, after Alice and John returned to them, and Jamie and I came home," said Alice.

Mother Nature's voice answered in her head saying...'*Indeed, they did – and whilst living their lives they paved the way for all of this to happen. Things always happen for a reason, Alice...and many times in life what may have seemed unimportant at the time will be some of the most significant events that transpired, once you look at the whole picture.*

Alice smiled again, and a warm feeling came over her as she remembered Albert the day she shook the dust off her one and only dress back in 1849.

"A penny for them..." offered Jamie, as he joined his sister and best friend.

Alice's smile broadened as she said, "I was just thinking about old Albert!"

"I would have loved to have met him," said Freddie.

"You would have loved both Albert and Doris," confirmed Jamie.

"You guys would have liked John and Alice, too..." replied Freddie.

"In a way, we did meet and like them," said Alice and Jamie at in unison, both bursting into laughter after Alice said,"Snap!"

"I wish Laura was here to witness this..." said Jamie wistfully.

"I have a feeling that Laura and the kids will join us at some point, and the wedding I was looking forward to can still go ahead...albeit slightly differently," encouraged his sister.

"I don't see how...just look at all this! If this is Leeds we are hundreds of years into the future," said Jamie, shaking his head.

"Let's just say...a voice in my head told me you would reunite," said Alice, mysteriously.

At that point, the very voice his sister was speaking of echoed in his own head...*Jamie Winters, hear me now – you have much to do, and if my plans are to be completed within the timescale needed, distractions must be few. All of your hard work and accomplishments now, and in the past, will be rewarded...so worry no more about your loved ones, for they are nearby.*

An elated smile came to Jamie's face, as he gave his sister a hug.

The rest of the people, led by Jasmine Lester, ventured out to where Alice, Freddie, and Jamie stood.

"This is the first day of the rest of our lives, Alice...what would you have us do with it?" said Jasmine.

"I would have you all run through the forest, shouting out loud how happy you are to be alive! I would have you dance, and sing, and play! Then, when you are too tired to dance, sing or play, we will retire to the shelter to sleep. On the morrow, we begin to build a new way of living!

All around the world bewildered but happy people were enjoying their day in the sunshine for the first time in a month. Planetwide, the collective minds of the survivors forgot their pasts. In this New World, all the things that meant so much to so many people were gone – money, property, possessions, petty jealousy...these were all part of a distant and long-forgotten past, and no longer held any importance. In this wondrous new Humanity, none of the aforementioned could exist...nobody would own anything, much less anyone. Now, there was no difference in skin colour, or tone. Differing languages would evolve and unfold into a new universal language, which would develop over the next ten years. Everyone could now understand what everyone else was saying. On a planet devoid of derision or hate, not one single person would ever be ridiculed for their beliefs, nor would they impress their religion upon anyone...because religion did not survive the Apocalypse. A universal love of nature was the spiritualism of the New World, and peace and tranquillity would reign upon this lush, green planet.

Chapter Two

Inside a cave within the Pennines – the backbone of England – at what used to be the divide between Yorkshire and Lancashire, stood a group of people, all ready to begin a new life. Keith, Josie, Debbie, and Garry Anderson took their first hesitant steps into their new surroundings. Following close behind were Sophie Narey, Steve Bingham, and Claire and Bernadette Hanson, with Craig and Thomas Bingham bringing up the rear. The entire group of friends had spent their last few hours in the cave packing everything that was there into rucksacks for the journey ahead of them.

This same scenario was echoed throughout the planet as the survivors who'd been saved by Atkinson's Warriors for passing over by the Reaper began their journey to a preordained place. Upon their arrival, they would join with a community of people saved by Nature Industries. The same look of astonishment and wonder was on each and every face of the ones who had been saved, and within, a galvanized determination to seek out other survivors. The mass exodus from the caves was underway.

In the Other Realm, a meeting was taking place between Atkinson, Dewhirst, Smith, Tamara, and the Warriors. It was being held in Dewhirst's chambers, and was informal. The reasons for this gathering were much happier than the previous one held there.

"A time of rest and recuperation is upon us. There is no reaping to be done in the immediate future, so for the first time in a very long while, we have all earned some freedom. You can spend this as and where you wish...Within the Other Realm, the Realm of Nature, or the Plane of Existence. Now, who wants to go where?" asked Atkinson.

Tamara was first to speak. "I will visit the Realm of Nature, and offer my services to Mother."

"I am sure she will more than appreciate your offer, Tamara," agreed Atkinson.

After a quiet chat with Gavin, Sarah said, "We would like to go to the Plane of Existence and offer our help...It will be a way of extending our earthly lives a little longer."

"I think I will join them, as I too will be able to help," offered John Smith.

"What about you two?" asked Atkinson, as he looked at Dixie and Paul.

"We will remain here in the Other Realm, spending time getting to know our daughter, and preparing for the arrival of our new baby," answered Dixie.

"And you Dewhirst, what are your plans?" asked Atkinson.

"I will stay here and devise a new way of working together. I also have much scribing work to do, as the insect and animal kingdoms are not blessed with five generations of death-free status."

"I will also remain for a while, then, to help with the initial stages...then, I will join Tamara. I will, however, keep in touch with all of you whilst you enjoy this time of R & R. All that is left for me to say is, have fun, my fine Warriors!" Atkinson slightly bowed his head, drawing the meeting to a close.

Meanwhile, Jack Howard and Simone Baudelaire had readied the Scottish contingent of survivors chosen by Nature for their long journey South. Wendy Walters prepared the Welsh saviors under her safe keeping for their journey Northeast, and the Southern contingent had already begun their epic journey due North.

These travellers would converge just West of Leeds, then together they would navigate the last 10 miles to where Alice Winters-Chambers and her team awaited. Depending upon where they were journeying from, the scattered cave survivors would find the nearest group, steadily increasing the number of voyagers on a daily basis, until all were safely united within the new community.

In the old Centre of Leeds, Michael Lester, Jamie Winters, and Freddie Chambers were surveying land near the river to find a place in which to build their community. They required an area that was flat and higher than the river, just in case it was still prone to flooding, as it used to be. As the three men stood in a wooded area where all the trees seemed to be of the same thickness, Michael pointed out a tree that had been uprooted...the root systems of this tree was very shallow – perfect for clearing a space for the log cabins.

Jamie walked over to the river. The water was moving at a good rate – not too fast or slow; it was as if everything had already been arranged for them...which, unbeknownst to them, it had. Satisfied, Jamie returned to where Michael and Freddie stood. As the three would-be civil engineers marked out where the first log cabins should be, and how many trees would be needed to build the structures, euphoria fell upon them. This was a feeling they had never experienced before...a togetherness and a belief in each other's abilities. Jamie was the first to speak. "I don't know about you guys, but I'm feeling positively elated about this place!"

"I'm getting that, too!" echoed Michael.

"This will be perfect – there is just a great atmosphere about the place!" agreed Freddie.

"Let's hurry back and report our findings to Alice!" suggested Michael.

The trio returned to find Alice, Jasmine, and Mina speaking with the rest of the group. All three found a place amongst their friends, and listened to what Alice had to say. Alice watched them settle in, and began to speak. "Today, we shall commence building...our wonderful surveyors have returned, and we will hear from them presently. This community will be one that runs on love, and peace, with everyone lending a hand. When something needs to be done, we will do it as a whole; that way, we grow closer as a community, and the work is done in a fraction of the time. We have much to accomplish, but all the time in the world to achieve it. I, for one, am looking forward to this challenge...and shall be working alongside you. In the past, I paid people to build my housing projects, whereas now there is no money with which to pay for labour. We are doing this because we want to – and to encourage community spirit. Now, I would like for us to hear from our surveying team."

Michael stood, and made his way through the gathered group up to Alice's side.

"We have found the perfect spot – I say 'we' found it, but I think something guided us there...it is near the river, and has everything the community needs."

A voice entered Alice's head...*I may have given them a gentle nudge in the right direction.* Alice smiled, happy in the knowledge that Mother Nature was still helping.
"We ask that everyone grab a tool from the shelter and come with us...as soon, that is, as Alice has finished speaking to you," offered Michael.
"Hey – I'm finished! Let's get off our bums, grab some tools, and get started, folks!" enthused Alice, the broadest smile adorning her face, her excitement clear to see.

Jamie went to the locker and started handing out tools needed for the day's work. All fifty people then walked to where the building site would be.

In the Pennines, the scenery on the way to Leeds looked very different to the way it had on the journey the Anderson family made to reach the cave...this was a completely transformed landscape. As soon as they vacated the cave, they found themselves in a pine forest...not the harsh scrubland of before, which had only been fit for sheep grazing. Sophie Narey, astonished, pointed out that not one sheep could be seen. As they stood in shocked silence, they noted that no birdsong could be heard either.

Josie recalled the stark contrast between the beautiful ramble through the woods they were enjoying now to the terrifying journey from their house to the cave. The Martian-like environment was gone...the volcanoes had gone; all she could see now was Nature's beautiful design. As they walked, Sophie was writing in her journal, recording the fresh smells and wonderful landscape that she was experiencing. As she wrote, her quill ran out of ink. To her and everyone else's astonishment, upon her shoulder appeared a fairy.

"Hello, Sophie!" said the tiny being, with an adorable smile.
"You...are a fairy?" gasped Sophie.
"Didn't Mother foretell of appearance?" asked the fairy.
"Well...yes, she did, but I didn't think that fairies..."
"Existed?" interrupted the fairy.
Sophie nodded her bewildered head.
"There will be many things to come you all will have to get used to...especially when the animals return," instructed the beautiful little creature.
"What is your name?" asked Sophie, unable to contain the smile that now lit up her face.

The fairy did a little curtsy, and said, "My name is Delphinium."

"What a beautiful name! You don't look like the fairies in the books I've read," said Sophie.

"Mother placed that image into Mr. Disney's imagination so that if anyone ever went looking for a fairy they, would be looking for Tinkerbell. As you can see, I am different. May I replenish your quill for you?" offered Delphinium.

"Yes, please!" smiled Sophie.

Delphinium touched Sophie's quill and the ink was replaced. She then sat on Sophie's shoulder.

"Are you going to stay with me?" marvelled Sophie.

"I would love to...but that is up to you. I am your personal fairy, and will appear when needed."

"Oh, yes! Please stay with me!"

The little fairy flew up from Sophie's shoulder, kissed her cheek, and said, "I am with you until you want me to leave."

"I'm never going to want you to leave – we will be friends forever!"

Delphinium fluttered up to a tree branch, plucking a bright pink flower from it and returning to Sophie, offering the gigantic blossom to her new friend with open hands. Sophie gently took the tiny bloom and placed it in her hair. Delphinium flew up to the flower, and touched it with her tiny hand. The blossom grew to a size where it could be seen majestically gracing Sophie's hair. The scene was magical; everyone around them witnessed the event, and all smiled as a joyous feeling engulfed them.

Delphinium flew back down and nestled on Sophie's shoulder. Sophie began to write in her journal everything that had just taken place. The group of ten humans – and one delightful fairy – continued on their journey to where Leeds once stood.

On the expedition from Scotland, Simone and Jack were discussing how they'd found themselves to be where they were.

They discovered they both had a lot in common; they bore the same love of healing the Earth, and both were born leaders...people who could handle anything that was put their way.

"What part of Scotland do you hail from?" asked Jack Howard.

"I'm not from Scotland; I am German, but I was living in Edinburgh."

"Oh, wow! I love...sorry, loved Germany. I used to go to the Goth festivals there."

"Me too! I loved the German Goth festivals...but I also loved the Whitby Gothic Weekend too. Whereabouts in the world are you from, Jack?" asked Simone.

"A month ago, you wouldn't have needed to ask me that," laughed Jack. "I'm from Scotland – but I think I was supposed to be in a shelter in London. I didn't make it there, because I was on my way to see the Prime Minister when the apocalypse broke," he continued.

"Whoa! Are you famous, Jack?"

"Me, famous? Why do you ask that?"

"You were going to see the Prime Minister..."

"Oh, I see...no, Simone, I'm not famous. I was Head of Meteorology, and as such, I was on my way to inform the Prime Minister of what was occurring all around the planet."

"A very important job, then."

"Not as important as my new job..."

"What is your new job?"

"I will show you – come with me," invited Jack.

The copse of the forest they were travelling through was dark. Jack lifted his arm, and said, "Three jewels lighter." Instantly that area of the forest was illuminated. Simone's eyes opened wide, as she witnessed the magic Jack had just performed.

"It isn't magic, Simone...it is Earth power."

"You read my mind!" said an astonished Simone.

"Can you not read mine?"

"You like cats?"

"See – you can read my mind too!"

"Wow...I really can!"

The two new friends continued their journey South with the rest of Simone's troop.

In Wales, the first day of travel was going well. The path that was set was mostly flat, and although made of dirt, was comfortable underfoot. The mood of the Welsh contingent was upbeat. There were no regrets for leaving their country, as the boundaries between nations were no more. The fierce patriotic stance that most English, Scottish, Welsh, and Irish people bore had dissipated. This had nothing to do with loving their particular country less...their patriotism had simply been removed, and a total acceptance of each other now existed.

Wendy Walters lead the group as she made her way towards the next beacon. The fourty-nine people following her began to sing – but it wasn't a Welsh standard, such as 'Men of Harlech', it was a song no-one had heard before, but they all seemed to know the words. This song spoke of their epic journey, and a new way of living. As Wendy was walking, she felt a small hand slip into hers. Surprised, she looked to her left, and saw someone she didn't recognise. "Who are you?" smiled Wendy.

"Hello, Wendy...I am Joytrium! I have been helping your followers to sing! I am your Muse, sent to you by Mother Nature."

"My Muse?" marvelled Wendy, her smile broadening.

"Yes! I am the one who has been placing the beacons that you follow. I have also been helping you with the decisions that you make."

"I thought I was making those decisions..." answered a perplexed Wendy.

"You do make the decisions, Wendy...I merely 'inspire' you to make them," beamed Joytrium.

Wendy giggled, and asked, "Is life going to be like the fairy tales I read as a child? I dreamed of riding unicorns, and playing with fairies in a world of wonder and magic..."

"Most of what you dreamed of as a child was you seeing the future...a future that you now march towards. But have a care Wendy – unicorns can be cranky when they are hungry, so if you come across one, always offer a tasty treat, then all will be fine," advised Joytrium.

The conversation with her Muse compelled Wendy Walters to walk faster towards her destination. The peaceful life she had always dreamed of – but which eluded her – was awaiting her in what used to be Yorkshire. She turned to her brood and shouted, "Best foot forward, lovely people! Something wondrous awaits."

Intrigued everyone quickened their pace to keep up with Wendy.

The journey North was well underway, as each member of the Southern contingent took turns leading the way. There were fourty-nine people in all. Just in front of them, a shadowy figure carrying a lantern guided their way. This stranger had only recently joined the group, and not made contact. He simply walked ahead of everyone, and never looked back.

Philip Tiple, an artist from Southampton, quickened his pace to catch up with the guiding angel, as his curiosity was piqued.

"I'm no Angel."

Philip was rattled by the gruffness of the figure's voice. Clearing his throat, he regained his nerve, and bravely asked, "Who are you? Why do you lead our way?"

The cloaked figure looming over him abruptly stopped, turning to the human standing at his side. "It matters not...you still live, so that means I am in human form." The cloak fell to the ground, revealing its wearer as none other than John Smith. A cold shudder passed through Philip's body – similar to the one he'd felt when he grasped the hand of the winged creature back in the shelter – but this sensation was the total opposite of what he experianced before.

"Fear not...I have a cold handshake, but my intentions are warm. I journey North to meet up with a friend, and unlike you fine people, I know the way. I am going to guide you there, as the man who should be here was unavoidably delayed, but will be joining you in Yorkshire."

John Smith released his grip, and an uneasy Philip Tiple said, "But...who are you?"

"You now live in a magical world – a world totally different to the one you knew. Science plays no role in this world, and Life and Death are simpler to understand. Through Mother Nature, I give life; through Atkinson, I take it away. For 600 moons there will be no Death, so the Reaper can choose what he wants to do with his spare time. I have chosen to travel to Yorkshire, to visit a friend."

With a shocked look on his face, Philip Tiple returned to his friends, leaving the strange being alone with his lamp.

As Smith walked on, Atkinson – invisible to the group following– joined him. "I forgot to tell you something..." he began.

"What's that?" quipped Smith, not even flinching at Atkinson's sudden arrival.

"Have you noticed things seem a little...odd at the moment?"

"I have indeed...people don't seem to like me...is that because they know what we have just done?"

"It's a bit simpler than that. When you want to converse with humans, you now have to think, 'Change to human'. You must do this because they will see you as a Reaper if you begin to speak without thinking."

"Good lord! I must have scared that poor man silly! Come to think of it, I can't actually remember what I said to him."

"You will have spoken frankly about Reaping...which could be why the poor fellow turned a whiter shade of pale. I suggest thinking 'Change', then starting again with him, you might find it helps. I'll see you later, Smith," waved Atkinson, as he returned to the Other Realm.

John Smith thought *human,* then walked back to the group. As he did he noticed the tatty cloak lying on the ground. Everyone stopped in their tracks as Smith approached them. But this wasn't the 'Grim Reaper' that Philip had just warned them about – this guy looked like an accountant. A few titters could be heard.

"Hello!" greeted Smith cheerfully. "I hope you don't mind me walking with you! I am travelling to Yorkshire, so I can meet up with my partner Tom, and I wondered if I could tag along with you fine people?"

Philip crept back up to John Smith and studied him closely "You seem to have changed...something about you is different," said Philip, suddenly doubting himself.

"Sorry about that..." said John looking down and kicking some lose dirt. "I didn't know if you guys were friendly, so I tried to make myself look fierce and kept my distance from you...what I said was true, though."

"What!?" yelped Phillip, backing away.

"I do know the way...and can show you," said John Smith with a cheerful smile.

Phillip burst into laughter as the thought of talking to the Grim Reaper evaporated...and was replaced with the worry about staying awake during a conversation with this guy.

The Southern contingent – now 50 strong – carried on their march North.

Back in Leeds, Michael, Jamie and Freddie saw to the distribution of pickaxes, shovels, wheelbarrows, and saws to all 47 people. Once these tools were handed out, the entire group of 50 headed to where they planned to build the foundation of their new future. It didn't take long to arrive at the spot chosen by the three men earlier that morning. The group looked about themselves; there were no areas that seemed large enough in which to construct anything.

"How can we build here? There is no space –just trees –as far as the eye can see," observed Glenn Simpson.

"That is the beauty of this place, Glenn…as we remove the trees, the space they occupied will be freed for construction. That way, we save on the undue labour of moving the trees," informed Michael Lester.

"Firstly, we will clear an area large enough to build six cabins…that way, we will have plenty of space in which to work. As a matter of fact, that can be our first task – so let's see how deep these roots are. Who's good at climbing trees?" asked Jamie Winters.

"I am!" shouted Linda Harper excitedly, jumping up and down with her hand in the air.

"Yep…I can vouch for that," quipped her brother Tom.

Freddy walked over to Linda, and with a broad smile on his face said, "I'm going to tie this rope around your waist. Can you shimmy up that tree, then when you are just above halfway, tie the rope around it and come back down?"

"Easy, peasy!" said Linda confidently, as she grabbed the first branch and like a little monkey, quickly made her way to the appointed area and tied off the rope, then climbed back down. The whole process took less than 5 minutes.

"Well done, Linda! Now, stand over there and save your strength, for there are many trees to fell today if this works," said Michael.

Linda stood to one side, while twenty men and women grasped the rope, and in unison, began to pull. To everyone's amazement, the ground released the roots of the tree, and it fell to the sound of snapping branches.

"Did you see that?" marvelled Freddie open-mouthed.

"Those roots are only 18 inches deep…how can that be?" mused Michael.

"I have a feeling they won't remain that depth, once we have what we need," said Alice, with a knowing smile.

"In that case, let's take advantage of the situation, and fell as many of these trees as we can!" enthused Jamie.

Linda found herself climbing more trees than she had since she was a youngster...and enjoying every minute of it.

Everyone was divided into six groups; twenty people were pulling down trees, thirteen were trimming off branches, three pairs were using double-handed saws and cutting logs, and ten were clearing the shallow topsoil down to the bedrock – which was only 18 inches deep, and extremely loose. One very nimble individual – Linda – climed and tied the rope around each tree.

The saws were incredibly sharp and easy to use, and cut through the felled trees with a minimum of effort. Their trunks were fashioned into logs of 24 and 12 foot lengths, which was the width and depth of each cabin, respectively. Over time, they would of course be able to enlarge them as needed.

At the end of the first day, a clearing down to the bedrock of 100 square feet and two stacks of different lengths of logs sat proudly in the forest, as the group of 50 made their way to the river to freshen up. When they arrived, there was a momentary uncomfortable silence, as no-one knew quite how to go about removing the day's grime in everyone else's company.

Alice strode forward and removed every stitch of her clothing, walking into the river and beginning to bathe. The water felt deliciously cool, and refreshing. Instinctively, all 49 disrobed and joined her, as the stigma of undressing in front of others disintegrated. The sounds of splashing and laughter could be heard as Viktoria Harper said to her wife, Linda, "Can you imagine the headlines? 'Chief Superintendent Viktoria Malik bathes naked...in public'!"

Linda laughed, and added, "And in front of Sergeant Glenn Simpson!"

Both ladies chuckled enjoying the freedom they felt at that moment in time.

JOHN PAUL BERNETT

Chapter Three

Just like the people of Yorkshire, the travellers from Scotland, Wales, Southern England, and all the separate caves were settling down for the evening as they were treated to a magnificent sunset. As the evening meals were prepared, a final burst of orange-yellow light filled the sky, delighting their senses.

In what used to be Leeds, Alice had decided that all cooking would be done outside, over an open fire, to acclimate people with cooking that way again. Within the shelters, they had been using microwave ovens – so the sooner she could wean them off those, the better. Alice herself took charge of the first open-plan natural kitchen, as on the journey back from the river, her people had collected food from the ground and trees. She used the wooden utensils and pottery cookware from the shelter. Everything within the abode had been fashioned with this in mind; the wood grew all around them, and the clay was readily available, so it would be easy to replace them as they wore out.

That first unforgettable feast was minted potatoes with carrots and cabbage. Protein was provided by a mixture of different nuts. As Alice, Jasmine, Mina, Freddie, and Jamie helped prepare then dish out the food, Alice thought that for the time being, this was the best way to eat...together, all in one place.

After enjoying her meal, Alice said to Freddie, "Can we build a kitchen and cafeteria first?"

Freddie brought Jamie and Michael into the conversation. "What do you think about building what Alice has asked for first?" Both Michael and Jamie thought it a great idea, so the next day's project would need sorted.

Sitting next to Michael was a woman named Julia Naylor. After overhearing their conversation, she said, "I can draw the plans up for you if you'd like, it's what I used to do for a living."
All three guys smiled as Michael asked, "Can you design a kitchen with dining room to hold 200+ people that we can construct with the materials we have?"

"Yes I can, do we have any drawing equipment?" asked Julia.

"Everything you need is in the main room of the shelter," said Alice, after Mother Nature informed her of the fact.

"Thank you, Alice! It will be a pleasure working for you again."

"You mean working with me? I don't understand...please forgive me, but have we worked together before?"

"It's the only memory I seem to have brought with me...my business partner Stuart Pierce was a builder, and he did the renovation of one of your hostels, whilst I drew the plans for the conversion," informed Julia.

"Oh, wow! Yours was the best design of all the hostels I had built! I wanted to meet you to thank you personally, but my schedule at the time wouldn't allow it. How wonderful it is to finally meet you!" enthused Alice as she embraced Julia.

"The pleasure is all mine!"smiled Julia, as she washed her plate in the water barrel, then went inside.

Upon arriving in the main room, she was astounded to find a state-of-the-art drawing desk, with everything she would need to work out her calculations for the different sizes of buildings required. She quickly sat down, and began to plan out the commune of the future.

Outside, Alice heard Mother Nature's voice once again. *The drawing equipment will remain only until Julia has designed the buildings you will need...it will disapear as soon as she has finished. These drawings must be kept safe for future generations to follow. There is an architect en route from Wales who will be able to transform those plans into your new community...so begin with your cafeteria, until he arrives.*

"Thank you, Mother," said Alice out loud.

Nighttime fell across the land and Simone, Jack, and the Scottish contingent settled down after having their own meals made from Nature's bounty. To their surprise, Nature had supplied material from which makeshift hammocks could be fashioned.

The trees where they had come to rest were all about eight feet apart from one another, so it wasn't long before fifty makeshift beds were erected and filled with tired travellers.

Wendy Walters had found things much the same with her brood. Joytrium – Wendy's muse – had informed her that this would occur, so as soon as they found the stack of material to make bunks with, Wendy called time on that day's march.

The food from the rations carried within the backpacks of the travellers was prepared. Not long after sunset, they retired to bed en mass, looking forward to the next day's journey. Wendy sighed and laid back in her bunk, taking stock of all that had transpired. A smile came to her lips as she heard Joytrium whisper, "You are an inspiration to these lovely people, Wendy."

"I love my people," she answered without hesitation.

"Of course you do...that was one of the many reasons Mother chose you...your ability to love unconditionally."
Joytrium leaned over Wendy's hammock, and kissed her cheek. Wendy smiled once more, then drifted off to sleep.

The travellers on the road North had eaten as well, and were all sitting around a campfire discussing the experiences that had led them to this point in their lives. John Smith had decided to take charge of this group of people from all walks of life – none of whom had ever held power over anyone else. He stood and addressed the assembly.

"My friends...may I have your attention, please? My name is John Smith, and I am here to help you wonderful people. I can answer any of your questions, and I will lead you to your destination. I know some – if not all of you – are still wondering what happened...and why such a great deal of time seems to have passed in the outside world whilst you spent your month in the shelter. These – and many other questions I will answer for you."

"Where did you come from?" asked Dougie Squires, a plumber from what used to be Southend.

"I am from another Realm of Existence; you will all be instructed about this upon our arrival in Yorkshire."

"Why do we have to go to Yorkshire? We should stay in London," added Martin Crowther, a tailor from London.

"Because London doesn't exist anymore. Your salvation lies in the hands of Alice Winters-Chambers – who, as we speak, has begun building a commune in Leeds in which you all can live," answered Smith.

"Why should we trust you? We don't even know you!" interrupted Martin Crowther.

"Do you trust the people you travel with?" asked Smith pointedly.

"Yes."

"Why do you trust them when you don't know any of them?"

Martin pondered this a while then said, "I take your point."

The conversation died down as the nighttime insects began their chatter. All of Mother Nature's primary humans fell peacefully to sleep. All, that is, except one...who, like Jack Howard, didn't make it to a shelter. Sophie Narey was writing in her book, covering that day's march towards an unknown destination.

"It's not an unknown destination – I know exactly where you are going!" boasted Delphinium, as she nestled up to Sophie's ear.

"Well, little Miss Clever-Clogs – where are we going?" giggled Sophie.

"We are going to a place that used to be called Leeds."

"Hey...I used to live near there! I have a friend who works in the City Centre...he helps his wife run a Gothic clothing shop there," smiled Sophie.

"You had a friend there. I am afraid he, along with almost everyone else from that city, is long gone," frowned Delphinium.

"Oh, yes...I had forgotten. All this will take some getting used to, Delphinium."

"That's why I am here – to keep you happy! We must think of the future now, and not live in the past. It's time to rest...are you ready to see how you will sleep from now on?" whispered Delphinium.

"What do you mean?"

Delphinium flew down to the ground at the side of Sophie, then the tiny fairy grew to Warrior size. She effortlessly picked an astonished Sophie up in her arms, then flew into the treetops. Once there, she nestled into the soft branches at the very top, and wrapped her glimmering wings around Sophie. Sophie's tired eyes looked up with love and wonder at the magnificent fairy that was cradling her as she fell into a deep sleep.

"Sleep well, Sophie," said Delphinium, as she tightened her wings and wrapped them protectively around her human planting a gentle kiss on her forehead.

A soft rain fell through the night, but daybreak was a spectacular event. A light mist was clearing from the forests as all the travellers awoke.

The Anderson family and friends were not the only cave-dwellers heading for Yorkshire...in all, there were around 100 making their way there. Once everyone had reached their destination, the commune would be 300 strong.

Alice was only aware of the 200 people which had been saved within her shelters, so her calculations were based upon that figure. Whilst she pondered on how many others might turn up two of them arrived.

"Hello Alice!" said one of them.

"Sarah! What are you doing here?"

"Gavin and me thought we would lend a hand."

"Gavin and I," corrected Tom Harper, as he came over to where his friends stood.

"Hello, Tommy!" yelled Sarah.

"Hello, old boy," greeted Gavin.

"Hello guys! I am so glad to see you! I'm even glad to see you, Gorezilla..." quipped Tom, as Viktoria, Linda, and Glenn joined the happy reunion.

"Awww! Thank you, Tommy!" gushed Slabgirl.

"My name is Tom."

"Whatever."

"It's good to see that not everything has changed," giggled Linda to Viktoria.

In fact, everyone there was glad to see the new couple, and not one of them retained the knowledge that they were otherworldly Immortals that had helped save them. All, that is, except Alice. She knew exactly who they were, and was delighted that they'd arrived, just as Mother Nature had said they would. Gavin looked at Alice, and in thought transference said, *We are at your disposal, Alice.* Alice smiled, and returned a thought to Gavin...*How can we fail when we have Mother Nature and Atkinson's Warriors helping? I am so glad you are here!*
Gavin and Sarah both beamed at Alice.

Simone Baudelaire and Jack Howard had already stirred their travellers and were on the move. It seemed as time passed, the eagerness to reach Yorkshire increased. Just like the people in Wales, they were following beacons that guided their way. As the two new friends walked, someone nestled in between and linked arms with both of them.

"Hello, guys! Isn't it a beautiful morning?"

"Who are you?" asked a bewildered Simone.

"I am Peacetrium...your Muse, Simone."

"My Muse?"

"Yes – Mother Nature sent me to help you."

"Thank you! It is nice to meet you! This is Jack," said Simone.

"I know...everyone knows Mr. Jack Howard! He is the one chosen to receive Mother's gift. It's an honour to meet you, Jack Howard!" smiled Peacetrium.

"So...Muses exist as well? This just keeps getting better and better," said Jack, wearing a huge smile.

"Of course we do! how else would you make all these brilliant decisions without a gentle nudge from my sisters and I?" said Peacetrium, crossing her arms.

Jack snorted to himself as he walked on with his friend and her Muse.

From the treetops in a forest within what used to be Yorkshire, a giant fairy opened her wings to reveal a sleeping Sophie Narey. Sophie opened her eyes and stretched. After a very long yawn, she said, "It wasn't a beautiful dream! You are still here, and I am awake!"

"I will always be here, Sophie...shall I take you down to the pond to bathe?"

"That would be very nice," agreed Sophie.

Delphinium flew down to join the Andersons and their friends, who were already in the pond bathing. Sophie whispered into Delphinium's ear, "They are all naked..."

"So are you, Sophie," answered Delphinium.

Sophie looked down in surprise. "So I am! Well, I suppose I had better join them!" She gleefully ran into the pond and splashed around with everyone else, without a care for her or their nakedness. When everyone had finished freshening up, there was no rush to dress; time was spent leisurely drying themselves, and helping one another. Smiles all around was the order of the day, as the two Anderson parents rallied everyone to begin walking again towards their goal.

John Smith had never spent as much time – or been so personal – with as many people, nor had his attire ever been so bold. The Grim Reaper was standing quite naked in a river with 49 humans. A small grin crept across his face and he blushed, as he thought about bathing like this with Tom Harper. The splashing and merriment of the London contingent was mirrored to the Northwest, as, for the first time in her life, Wendy Walters shared a skinny dip with 49 other people. Even further North, Simone, Jack, and 48 others from Scotland had already discovered that wonderful experience.

The three groups that were journeying from the South of England, Scotland, and Wales all had the same distance to travel. Mother Nature made this possible by creating the walkways her Muses were using. The Southern contingent was traveling from Dorking, South of London. The Welsh were journeying from Swansea, in South Wales, and the Scots from Edinburgh. The walkways were set as the crow flies – consecutively 180 miles, 180 miles, and 160 miles long. The twenty-mile difference was made up by a slightly curved walkway for the Scots. At a steady pace, walking 8 hours a day, it would take them six days to converge just West of what used to be Leeds.

The Welsh and Scots with their Muses, and the Southern English with their Immortal marched for 8 hours each day, eating and resting at night. The six days passed very quickly, as the three groups came across no obstacles in their paths, nor experienced any problems walking; not even one blister was caused during the entire journey to Yorkshire. Friendships had been made along the way, and all three contingents' ranks swelled, as cave survivors joined their happy throngs.

The leaders of all three groups could now hear voices before them as they neared one another. Instinctively, Simone, Wendy, and Smith knew they had reached the merger point...which meant they would meet Alice Winters-Chambers before nightfall.

Chapter Four

Tamara arrived within the Realm of Nature. It was hard to believe, that this was her very first visit. On arriving, the first being she came upon was the Goddess herself, who opened her arms to welcome her.

"Welcome to my realm, daughter..."

"I am honoured to be here," answered Tamara, lowering her head.

"The honour is mine, welcoming the first-born female."

"First-born female?" said a confused Tamara.

"Yes...you were the first, your sister was second."

Tamara's face still showed confusion as Mother Nature explained. "I bore my man-child through Atkinson; I bore my women-children through Dewhirst."

"This means I now have full knowledge of my entire family! Thank you, Mother! Does it also mean I have had a thousand-millennia-long love affair with my brother?"

Mother Nature chuckled as she said, "No, my child...Atkinson's DNA is completely different to yours. You must remember I am nothing like the females you have met before. When I mated with Dewhirst, I was a very different being to the one I was when I mated with Atkinson – even though both events were only one hour apart."

"So...you were pregnant with Atkinson at the same time you were pregnant with me?" marvelled Tamara.

"I was pregnant with all four of you at the same time. I kept two back, to see how you and Atkinson's child would get along."

Tamara was taken aback. "Four of us?"

"Yes...after 6 of our moons – which in human terms was many years – I gave birth to another daughter for Dewhirst, and another son for Atkinson."

"Who was this other son? I wasn't aware of his existence," said Tamara.

"That is because Atkinson put him to death as soon as he was born. He feared two sons might pool their strength and rise up against him. This – along with other things – drove a wedge between us...a wedge that has only recently been removed."

"Dewhirst was right to keep this to himself...I don't know how my lover would feel if he knew about it," said Tamara, looking sad.

"I do know about it, and am perfectly at ease with it. Truth be told I have always known," said Atkinson from behind her.

Tamara spun round in shock, as she had not realised he was standing there.

"Hello, Mother," said Atkinson, bowing his head.

"It is good to have you here," smiled Mother Nature, responding in kind.

"How long were you standing there?" asked Tamara.

"Long enough to find out you've been cavorting with your brother, you kinky minx!"

"At least I didn't know about it...unlike you!" said Tamara with a giggle.

"Now that you are both here, shall we go and meet everyone?" suggested Mother Nature.

"Lead on, Mother," smiled Atkinson, placing his arm around Tamara.

In the Other Realm, Dixie and Paul were getting used to their life of ease. The refurbished house was now fully mind-operational, and everything was just a thought away. Having

Aquallia around all the time, looking as human as she possibly could, was wonderful for both parents. The whole family was looking forward to the new arrival, which was due very soon.

Paul Johnson asked his daughter what she had planned for the day.

"I am meeting my manatee, and we are going to play," announced Aquallia gleefully. With that, she ran to the balcony and leapt over the safety rail, performing a triple somersault and entered the water without a splash, instantly morphing into a mermaid.

"Clearly not going to help with the washing up, then..." quipped Paul Johnson.

Dixie shook her head at him, then thought, *Wash the dishes.* Elementals appeared in the kitchen and the pots were washed, dried, and put away in seconds. Dixie came and sat on Paul Johnson's lap, kissing him.

"Hmm...that was nice! Anymore where that came from?"

"Shall we go upstairs and see?" coaxed Dixie.

It didn't take long for her husband to stand, pick her up, and carry her upstairs. In the blink of an eye she was undressed, standing naked and heavily pregnant in front of him. Kissing her round tummy, he gazed up at her and said, "She will be beautiful, like you."

"He will be handsome, like you," corrected Dixie.

"Will he be a normal human boy?" asked Paul.

At this point, in the Realm of Nature, the Goddess excused herself, as she had something to do that wouldn't take long.

In the Other Realm, the Goddess appeared in front of the naked Dixie and Paul.

"Hello, children...do excuse my unannounced entrance."
Paul did his usual cover-up that he had perfected whenever Tamara arrived.

"Paul, my dear, do not cover yourself. I don't see clothing on people, because it can interfere with their aura; I need to see a being's aura, so I can discern if their words are true…hiding yourself is of no use."

"You always see people naked?" gasped Johnson.

"I see them as I created them. The reason for my visit is to clarify something…your male child will be as human as possible. I have anguished over this ever since I gave my blessing for you to have another child. The only exception I have made is that he must be Immortal, and my reasoning is this – you both will be with Aquallia for all time. If your son was completely human, he would only be with you for about 70 Earth years, which would leave you grieving for him throughout all eternity…I cannot let that happen. Your son will be human in everything except life expectancy…I hope you understand why I did this," said Mother Nature.

Paul and Dixie not only understood the situation, they were thrilled with this wonderful news. They both bowed, and accepted gracefully. Mother Nature smiled and returned to Tamara and Atkinson, as Paul and Dixie recommenced making love.

Within the Other Realm sat Dewhirst, at his ornate desk. Whilst sending names and life numbers to the insect and arachnid Listmakers, he began configuring a system for Atkinson and Smith to work to upon their return to reaping. The old way of twenty-five-year administrations on the Plane of Existence would not be back in force for 1000 years, so modifications had to be made.

The old Tudor building had returned to its original place within the Other Realm, in the area where Atkinson and his Warriors battled the army from the Dark Realm. Mr. Braithwaite was still in charge of his small amount of clerks as he, too, prepared for the new bookkeeping of life beginning again.

All of the documentation regarding Humanity up to this point in time was in the process of being removed from the Tudor building, to be placed in the Great Vault of Extinction. This vault contained all the species Mother Nature had allowed to dominate her planet, but had eventually found herself at loggerheads with their way of existence. The new Humanity was a completely unique race of beings.

The Goddess of Nature desired a dominant species that would rule justly, leaning towards love – and not greed. Allowing Homo Erectus to mate with the visitors had proven to be their undoing, as hate and war flourished alongside love and understanding. She felt that if she began again, with intelligent humans having no thoughts of anger or war-like tendencies, she would stand a much better chance of achieving her goal.

As soon as Mr. Braithwaite completed rearranging, Dewhirst would be able to put the new system in place. This system would have no need of a Dark Realm to hold souls no longer receiving new life, as that type of entity would be extremely rare in the New World. At death, an unclean soul would be delivered straight to Nature as raw power, or to Aquallia, to be cleansed into a mermaid.

Dewhirst felt the new Reaper System would be a good one. He put down his quill and smiled.

Ten miles West of what used to be Leeds, three groups of people converged. The long trek was almost over, and salvation was in sight.

Simone walked up to Wendy, and the two women embraced. Jack Howard approached John Smith and shook his hand, then they, too, embraced. After the team leaders introduced themselves, all the gathered survivors mingled, the next several hours spent getting to know one another.

John Smith strolled over to the edge of the clearing where they were they stood, bringing everyone's attention to the trees behind him. To their amazement, they parted, revealing a straight path that led to what was formerly Leeds. Excitement buzzed within the now-extended group of people, as they all made their way towards Smith.

"Shall we?" smiled Smith, as he held out his arm in the direction the path was taking. He encouraged the others to follow him on the last leg of their epic journey.

Wendy, Simone, Jack, and Smith took the lead as everyone else followed, setting a path for the commune by the side of the River Aire in a wooded area that was once Leeds.

Within the Realm of Nature, Atkinson and Tamara were re-kindling old friendships. Mother Nature smiled as she enjoyed the merriment that was taking place. She beckoned Pan towards her.

"Isn't this wonderful?" beamed Mother Nature.

"It is how things should be," nodded Pan serenely.

The wondrous afternoon in the endless summer of the Realm of Nature soon passed, and the resting Reaper and his eternal Listmaker had eaten, drank, and definitely made merry as a quiet settled in.

Night fell, so Atkinson and Tamara retired to their holiday residence, deep within the Forest of the Night...A forest that existed in the beautiful nocturnal part of the Realm of Nature. This grove was home to the shadowy creatures of the night, and long-extinct nighttime songbirds filled the air with their dusk chorus. Badgers ambled in abundance all along the pathway and foxes foraged for food, as all manner of scurrying from the smaller creatures was taking place around them.

Tamara linked arms with Atkinson, and nestled into his side. The Reaper wore a smile of contentment, as he knew the legend of the place in which they now found themselves. The Forest of the Night was where Gods and Goddesses were conceived. This was where his father and Mother Nature created him...what would be the possibility of this same thing happening for him and Tamara?

Would you really want such a thing to happen my son? Mother Nature's voice rang loud and clear in Atkinson's mind.

Tamara's head turned as she looked straight at him.

"You are in my thoughts..." said Atkinson.

Tamara's eyes were full of tears, as they pleaded.

This question must be answered by you and you alone, Atkinson...I will be creating an even more powerful Immortal than yourself...a thing your father discovered to his own cost, continued Mother Nature.

Tears were now streaming down Tamara's beautiful face as she held her silence, her eyes looking longingly into Atkinson's own. Atkinson smiled at Tamara, and in thought said to Mother Nature, *I am not my father. Our son would grow into a loving God that respected his mother and father.*

So be it – your residence awaits, was the final thought from Mother Nature.

Tamara leapt into Atkinson's arms, and unable to put words together, she simply lavished kisses all over his face. Atkinson whisked her into his arms, walking towards the cave entrance that was now in front of them. As they entered, it was filled illumination, as the exquisite crystal formation within the cavernous room sparked into life. Upon entering, both changed to Warrior mode, minus the armour. Two giant magnificent Warriors stood within the cave – both aroused, both ready. Tamara finally found her tongue. "Is this why I wanted to come help Mother Nature?"

"I have been thinking about this for some time so I gave you a little jolt, shall we say."

Tamara smiled and kissed him once more. Two naked wood nymphs came to where they stood; one of them grasped Atkinson's hand whilst the other took hold of Tamara's. Both of them were ushered into separate rooms, where a multitude of wood nymphs awaited their arrival. Atkinson and Tamara were placed in pools of water...water so clear it looked like the pond was empty. The invigorating spa teased their skin as they entered.

Tamara's naked body was now bathed by the 12 wood nymphs as she lay still, being prepared for the most sacred of all things. She was kissed on her mouth, and that kiss astounded her. She opened her eyes to find Juliantrium, in wood nymph form, lying in her arms. Tamara pulled Juliantrium close, and kissed her once more. A feeling deep within Tamara's psyche awoke, and a warm empowerment took over her being. She had longed for this to happen all her life. Juliantrium's tongue made its way into her mouth, and at the same time, the tongue of another wood nymph found her clitoris. Tamara writhed in absolute ecstasy just as Pan entered the cave, joining his nymphs in the pool. Juliantrium moved behind Tamara, holding her with one arm as she stroked Tamara's hair with her other hand. Pan waded through the pool and came up to Tamara. He grasped her hips and gently placed his legendary phallus at the opening of her vagina. The normally vibrant, confident Tamara let all of what was happening sink in, as she had read many times in the Great Book about what was occurring at that moment in time.

In the other room, Atkinson was also being tended by twelve wood nymphs. The bathing had ended, and the frolicking had begun. He was being treated to pleasures beyond belief, as each took turns lavishing attention upon his erect penis with their waiting mouth. A beautiful nymph was probing his mouth with her tongue, whilst another two nibbled on his nipples.

Into the cave strode a Goddess...not in her crone years, but as a youthful and stunning woman. She was quite naked, and her beauty was the stuff that legends were made of. Her hair was long and golden and her figure womanly, with large, pert breasts, and child-bearing hips.

Atkinson looked upon the Goddess of Nature as his father had once seen her.

Remove that thought from your memory...I am many and never the same, said Mother Nature in thought. Atkinson lay back as the ancient beauty strode over him, lowering herself onto his awaiting, blood-enriched penis.

As Mother Nature and Pan, respectively, made love to Atkinson and Tamara, across the Plane of Existence every woman and man of straight sexuality suddenly felt the overwhelming need to copulate. This was a feeling they had no control over...it had to be fulfilled then and there. All over the world, humans were suddenly attracted to the nearest person of the opposite sex.

Back in the Realm of Nature, Mother Nature and Pan withdrew from the cave, as the first stage of creating a God was complete, Tamara's vagina held the essence of Pan, and Atkinson's erect phallus was moist and readied with the prepared DNA...the life-giving essence of the Goddess of Nature herself. The wood nymphs led Atkinson and Tamara back together. As soon as they saw each other, they ran into one another's arms, both needing sexual fulfillment there and then. As soon as they touched, they were straight on the large bed that had been provided, Atkinson unceremoniously parting Tamara's legs. This action was mirrored all over the Plane of Existence at exactly the same time. Atkinson's penis was now deep within Tamara, and all straight males on the planet was copying his every move. The lovemaking was animalistic and intense, and the throaty cries of Atkinson and Tamara reaching an explosive climax in unison were echoed all over the world.

In that one defining moment, the New Humanity began, and every woman who was able became pregnant, igniting the spark of life once again.

Within the Realm of Nature, Atkinson and Tamara lay back and fell into the most restful sleep they had ever known. Tamara had indeed helped Mother Nature and her Realm, more than she would ever know.

Chapter Five

In the commune, everyone was waking in a rather good mood. Viktoria Harper said to Linda, "What got into everyone last night? I have never seen so much cavorting going on at once!"

"I know...it did make our evening nice though," smiled Linda.

"Indeed it did...and did you notice when we made love to each other no one batted an eyelid?"

"Yes – I did notice that, and I love it!" said Linda.

Happy people all over the planet were rising to the same euphoric feeling, and overnight, the world's population had effectively grown from 700,000 to 1,050,000, as all babies conceived would be born per Mother Nature's plan. This was because all women were ovulating at the same time, their bodies in tune with the cycle of the moon, as it once had been.

Viktoria and Linda dressed, then joined the others for a refreshing breakfast of fruit and nuts. After eating, they all made their way to the future location for their houses...all that is, except Julia Naylor – she had spent the early hours of the night getting to know Michael Lester...intimately. She set about redrawing her designs for the homes, and added another bedroom to the plans. With dreams of a little Michael playing in her head, she ran out to him with her new drawings, wearing the broadest smile as she handed them over and she kissed him.

Michael smiled and said, "Thank you – for these, and for last night...I've never acted like that before!"

"You don't hear me complaining...that was the best sex I've ever had!"

"Me, too!" agreed Michael.

"I'll just go in and tidy the drawing desk, then I will follow you," said Julia.

Much to Julia's surprise, the desk was no longer there – and the knowledge of using it was fading fast. She shrugged her shoulders and ran out to be with the rest of her friends. It did not take long to reach the site they'd begun to clear the day before. The vison that greeted them was unbelievable; the entire area had been cleared, and all the logs needed for building were cut and piled into separate stacks by each dwelling's future location. There was also a very large area prepared, with enough logs to construct the kitchen and dining room.

Standing amidst all of this were Sarah and Gavin.

"How did you achieve all this work in such a short time and with just you two?" marvelled Michael Lester.

"It wasn't us...we've just arrived ourselves! Isn't it wonderful. I think Mother Nature must be helping..." said Sarah, with the fingers of both hands crossed behind her back.

Everyone was pleased to discover so much hard work was already done...everyone, that is, except Linda Harper – who was looking forward to another day of climbing trees. Alice Winters-Chambers came up behind Linda, resting her hands on her shoulders. "You have a full forest of trees that you can climb for the rest of your days!"

This revelation brought a wide grin to Linda's face, and Viktoria let out a giggle.

"What's so funny?" asked Linda, raising an eyebrow.

"Nothing...just a lovely vision of you hanging upside-down from a branch with your skirt falling over your head and your knickers showing..." smirked Viktoria.

"Chief Superintendent! I don't believe that is a suitable thought for such a high-ranking officer of the law!" said Linda with mock seriousness.

"I know...isn't it great?" said Viktoria, her giggle turning into a snorting laugh.

The two girls ran, hand in hand, down to the prepared area to sit with everyone else, whilst Michael, Jamie, and Freddie explained what their duties would be that day.

After the three men had gone over the plans, they smiled simultaneously, as they realised an extra bedroom had been sketched in. The general consensus was that this would be a good idea...especially after the night everyone had just enjoyed.

After reports had been delivered regarding the new buildings, and everyone was designated to a particular job, they all began working with relish. However, this wasn't like being employed – this was different. They were all filled with a wondrous surge of empowerment; they were the ones chosen to begin life anew...and that was better than any bonus one could offer for hard work before the Apocalypse had struck.

The buildings that the 52 people were working on were not just to build homes...they were shaping life itself, with each log that was fashioned and laid in place. The foundations of four dwellings soon took shape, as the finished logs were jointed and fixed together upon the bedrock. Four groups of 13 had prepared and laid the foundations two logs high, and the floor shape of the new dwellings could now clearly be seen.

As Alice and her brood were taking a break, voices could be heard wafting over the river. Alice and Jasmine Lester immediately stood up, both women held a finger to their lips and everyone grew quiet. Now, the entire group could hear voices, and they all stood and made their way to the river. When they arrived, a multitude of people were standing on the opposite bank; on the South side of the river was Alice and the people from the shelter, and on the North side stood Simone Baudelaire, Jack Howard, Wendy Walters, John Smith and the accumulated travelers which had joined them from the rest of her shelters in Great Britain. Many seconds passed by as time seemed to stop, and people stared at on another from either side.

Suddenly, Alice Winters-Chambers then ran into the water. Her actions were mirrored on the opposite side of the river as Simone, Jack, and Wendy came together like long-lost friends. Whilst John Smith was observing from his position on the North bank, he caught sight of Tom Harper. The two men's eyes met, and Tom Harper ran to the water's edge and dove in. John waded through the water with ease and met his lover in the middle. The two men embraced, then passionately kissed each other.

As the group leaders met in the middle of the river, treading water because of its depth, everyone else followed, jumping in without a care then swimming to meet each other. Not a single person stared at – nor gave a second thought too – the two men who had just found each other again. It was just taken as normal behaviour for two people in love to kiss in such a way.

Splashing and merriment abound as the entire group of people exited the river via the South bank. Once they were back on dry land, they made their way to where the commune was being built. Once there, they removed their wet clothing and hung it on trees to dry, without a worry for their modesty.

As the clothes dried, the discussions began. Tales of epic journeys were shared by each contingent. Many friendships were forged that day and work was set aside, as everybody took the time to get to know everyone else.

Away from the excited crowd, a small group of people had gathered. Sitting together in a circle were Alice Winters-

Chambers, Jasmine Lester, Mina Lester, Michael Lester, Jamie Winters, Freddie Chambers, Simone Baudelaire, Jack Howard and Wendy Walters. The first team leader meeting was taking place, and for a time, they simply chatted, getting to know one another. Soon, however, Alice felt the need to pass on to them the words of Mother Nature.

"Welcome, my friends, and thank you for delivering my children to this domain. I have placed within each of you the ability to govern with love and understanding. I have also given you an insight into what you will be doing over the coming months. It is up to you, my children, to keep the people happy, and to make them realise that they are very special. You have been tasked with keeping this momentum going; encourage them to work hard, play hard, and increase my population. You shall do this by example...you must never expect anyone to do anything that you are not prepared to do yourself. Respect must always be earned, and must go both ways, so they will feel part of a team − not part of a workforce. Each of you was handpicked to ensure this energy and drive continues within this part of the world. Have a care not to think that the positions you hold are ones of authority...they are not positions of power, but ones of guidance...and that guidance is granted to you through me. Each of you has certain abilities that will, over the ensuing months, come to the fore. Do not question these abilities − just accept them, and all will be well. Now, my children, go mingle with your people, make me proud of my choices."

Alice's eyes fluttered open, as she realised Mother Nature had just spoken to her friends through her. In her own words she then said, "These are the instructions of Mother Nature. We need to keep to them, and live our lives by them. People will be afraid, and be looking to us for answers to their questions...we are here purely to guide − not to rule." Alice smiled at the group of new friends, looking forward to working with them. She felt she already knew them, and that now they were here, the future was bright – and it most definitely was...this was a future to look forward to.

Michael, Jamie, and Freddie took Jack Howard to one side to discuss the current and future building plans. They showed him the schematics they had for the houses, and for the building venture that could now take place, thanks to the new arrivals. Jack looked at the plans, and a broad grin came to his face – he was about to indulge in building log cabins...something he himself had always dreamed of owning one day.

Everything that had happened to him – from the moment he found himself buried underneath a church in London, to when he was whisked away to live in a cave under Ben Nevis for the duration of the Apocalypse – had heightened his sense of awareness of everything around him. He shared the same enthusiasm that his three new friends were showing...but he had a secret – and now was the time to reveal it to this group of new-age builders.

Jack posed a seemingly-simple question. "Once your log cabins are complete, what are your plans for lighting after dark?"

"For the time being, the length of our waking hours will depend upon the span of daylight; we have tentative plans to grow seeds from which to make oil that can be burnt to produce light," said Michael.

"That's a good plan, but that would necessitate Humanity to begin using oil again. From the development of that first basic oil for producing light, we will end up on the same old path, ravaging the Earth for fossil fuels. What if I told you we could light all the new dwellings that we build with a power source that depends upon nothing other than raw Earth energy manifested through thought...the ability of which is in my hands?" asked Jack.

"This is a new world, and many a strange thing we have seen already. Such a power source would be a truly wondrous thing, setting us upon a path of discovery instead of one of disaster. I may have witnessed this power you speak of during a visitation from one of the winged creatures," said Jamie.

"Yes! That's exactly what I'm talking about! I have been granted this energy from Mother Nature, and it is now at our disposal," informed Jack.

"Could you give us a demonstration? Not that I'm doubting you at all! This development is truly exciting...it will afford us extra time through the evenings for planning, so that no daylight hours need be wasted!" enthused Freddie.

"It would be my pleasure! Come, follow me..." bid Jack.

The four men walked into the wooded area at the side of the building site. They entered an expanse where the tree canopy was such that very little light came through. Jack simply said, "Two jewels lighter."

The entire area they were in suddenly flooded with light. Jack's three new friends were astounded at what had just taken place. Michael quipped, "This just gets better and better!"

"We are so glad to have you on board, Jack! Could this the reason you were saved?" pondered Jamie.

"As far as I can tell, the reason I was spared is because of my meteorology skills. I used to be Head of Meteorology at the Met Office before the Apocalypse, and Mother Nature, in her infinite wisdom, believed knowledge of the weather would be a good asset to her New Age of Humankind. It was a good while after I was rescued when she visited me in the cave where I was that she bestowed this gift upon me," informed Jack.

"You can recall what you used to do...no one else seems to have retained their memories. Some know what they were but you remember everything – I wonder why?" mused Jamie.

The Met Office, and the knowledge of my skills, are all I have retained...I've no recollection of anything else," said Jack.

"Very interesting...come to think of it, I am much the same – I can recall becoming engaged, but my only other memories are of historical power supplies, and the setting in which I obtained them," said Jamie.

"Will you have to place this power into each dwelling every night?" asked Freddie.

"I wondered that at first, then asked Mother Nature if I was to be the Lamp-lighter of the New Age. I am glad to say the answer to that question is no. Once I have placed the light source within the building, it is there forever, and will illuminate when anybody walks into the room," informed Jack.

The group of four civil engineers finished their meeting with a positive outlook for the years to come.

At the same time the conversation between the engineers was taking place, Alice and Jasmine had been getting to know Wendy and Simone. In effect, these incredibly inspiring four women carried the responsibility of Humanity for what used to be Great Britain. Alice, however, also bore the responsibility for the entire planet.

A thought entered her head, as she said to her three companions, "Ladies, there will be one more joining us...I have seen her in my dreams, and as we speak, she is on a journey to where we are."

"Do you know when she will arrive, and what her name is?" asked Jasmine.

"She is known as Sophie Narey, and will be with us later today, or tomorrow. She will accompany me and will be my scribe, as she is the one who has been chosen to record the history of our New Beginning. All the history of humankind is gone...if you search your thoughts, you will find it difficult to recall what you did even one day before you entered the shelter. The new history of humankind will be seen through the eyes of a young woman, and written in a special journal provided by Mother Nature," said Alice.

Simone, Wendy, and Jasmine struggled to recall what they had been doing just prior to entering the shelters – the lives they had led, the people they had known...even the very place they had lived. Try as they might, they could not remember the events leading up to their arrival at the shelters. All three gaped at Alice, gobsmacked. Jasmine spoke first. "I can't recollect anything...It's as if my entire memory has been wiped clean!"

44

Simone and Wendy mirrored what Jasmine had just said.

"You are in this state so you may begin again – with no fear of the future, and no lamenting for the past. You are going to be very busy women, and those things would get in the way, so they have simply been removed," instructed Alice.

"In that case, the sooner Sophie gets here, the quicker you can embark upon your duties. These duties will take you all over the world, and whilst you are doing that, you'll know that your commune is in safe hands," assured Wendy Walters.

"You can rely on us to maintain everything in your absence," added Simone.

In the oceans of the Other Realm, Aquallia had been joyfully playing with her manatee when a strange feeling came over her. She suddenly had the urge to go home, sensing her mother was in distress. Without a word to her friend, Aquallia darted off in the direction of her parent's house. It didn't take long to reach her their dwelling, and as she drew near, she lifted her head towards the surface of the ocean and thrashed her tail. Breaking the surface at great speed, she morphed back into a girl, landing perfectly on the balcony, and running into the house dripping wet and panting for breath. She burst across the room into her mother's arms.

Dixie wore a pained expression due to the imminent arrival of Aquallia's brother.

"What's wrong mother?" asked Aquallia.

Dixie answered between pants of breath. "Your brother is about to be born, Aquallia...I'm just waiting for the midwife, who should be here presently."

"Why don't you go and make your mother a drink?" suggested Paul Johnson.

Aquallia smiled and ran to the kitchen to make her mother a beverage.

Within the Realm of Nature, the Goddess looked over at Tamara, and said, "Shall we go?"

Tamara stood and joined her, and both of them disappeared, reappearing at Dixie's side in the Other Realm.

Tamara grasped of Dixie's trembling hand and kissed her forehead saying, "Are you ready, my love?"

"I am ready," said a determined Dixie as she looked at Paul Johnson, then kissed him. Tamara guided Dixie to Mother Nature, and all three females climbed the steps into the bedroom. Once there, Dixie was helped onto the bed, and her clothing removed. Mother Nature placed her hand upon Dixie's swollen tummy, uttered a few incoherent words. Almost instantly, Dixie's contractions grew more intense, as the baby pushed its way towards the bright light.

As the child was Immortal, it did not need Atkinson or Smith to connect its mortal cord in the Realm of Death. Her labour was short, but intense, and the 9lb baby boy was born and handed to his doting parents.

Mother Nature smiled, as Tamara had delivered the baby perfectly. She congratulated Tamara, and bid the Johnsons goodbye as she left. Tamara sat in awe gazing at Dixie and Paul, and their two beautiful children Aquallia and Alex.

Whilst cradling the newborn, Tamara said, "Paul...you now have the son that you always dreamed of. Dixie...your family is beautiful, and complete. Aquallia...you now have a baby brother to play and grow with – All of you enjoy your family life together. Teach the boy well; the next 50 years belong to you, and you alone. I will see you in the office 50 years hence, when we all begin again with Death and Life."

Tamara smiled and gave all four members of the family a kiss...the children, upon their cheeks, and the parents, upon their lips. She smiled again sweetly, passing the baby back to Dixie. She gave a little wave of her hand, disappearing out of the Johnson's lives for the next half century.

The Johnson family moved outside onto the balcony, and the three eldest looked out upon the ocean, whilst the youngest simply slept. For the next 50 years, they were going to be a simple family, enjoying their simple life, in their beautiful home in the endless summer of the Other Realm. The magnificent evening sun slipped below the horizon as nighttime fell, and their new life began.

Tamara returned to the Realm of Nature and rejoined Atkinson. She threw her arms around him and kissed him passionately.

"What was that for?" smiled Atkinson.

"I'm just happy!"

"Then, so am I! I take it all went well with the Johnsons, and Paul now has his boy with legs that he can play football with," said Atkinson.

"Yes, he does...and what a beautiful family they make!" enthused Tamara.

"So, my dear, we appear to have 50 years to ourselves. What do you suggest we do with them?"

"I know a beautiful island inhabited only by your personal elementals. 50 years of pampering sounds quite acceptable to me," said Tamara, dreamily.

"As ever, my beautiful Listmaker – your ideas sound full of promise, and are always perfectly acceptable to me."

Atkinson and Tamara walked hand-in-hand to Mother Nature. As they arrived, she smiled and said, "My children...you are leaving the Realm of Nature?"

"The Listmaker and I have fulfilled the things we came here to do, and as such, we now beg your leave. We are going to spend 50 years on my island, enjoying its pleasures. These years since the turn of the new millennium have been some of the hardest in my existence, so I will use this time to recuperate, and give my Listmaker some much-deserved rest," said Atkinson.

"Leave this realm with my blessing, and my love. These last few years have been hard on you, Atkinson...but you fulfilled every task you were given, and the Reaper System is now as strong as it has ever been. The people of the New World, and indeed, we in the Realm of Nature, are forever indebted to your selfless actions. Go, my children, and take with you my dreams...we shall meet again when I bring you back to my realm to deliver the child that now grows within Tamara. The pregnancy will span four years through gestation to delivery – spend the rest of your time away from reaping to set the child on a true path," said Mother Nature.

Atkinson and Tamara bowed their heads and left the Realm of Nature, reappearing on his island in the beautiful turquoise sea of the Other Realm. There, they would spend the following 50 years enjoying their post-apocalyptic rest, until the Grim Reaper, his beautiful Listmaker, and their offspring were called into action once more in the New World.

Chapter Six
The Age of the Enlightened Human

Keith and Josie Anderson, and their party of young people who were saved within a cave in the Pennines, were happily walking through a wooded area when Keith raised his hand, and everyone stopped.

"I can hear voices," he said.

"So can I," said Josie.

Sophie Narey began writing in her little journal, and said, "I can hear it too – it is coming from just in front of us."

They suddenly realised they had reached their destination, and just through the trees lay the commune under construction by the survivors of Great Britain. They gingerly wended through the trees, peering down upon what would be their new home.

Alice was working one side of a double-ended saw when something distracted her, and she looked towards the edge of the commune. On seeing the group of young people, she smiled and walked towards them. She said "Hello!" and appeared to be looking for someone when Sophie Narey stepped forward and said, "Are you Alice?"

"I am indeed – welcome, everyone, to your new home! Especially you Sophie."

The two girls embraced. Alice knew her team was now complete, and things could start moving forward all over the world.

Everyone greeted the newcomers, and food and drink were made available to them after their long journey. The Andersons and their friends were the last of the saved people to arrive at the commune. The cave survivors had been steadily trickling in since the Scottish, Welsh, and Southern English arrived. Although the Anderson's journey had been amongst the shortest that any of the travellers had taken, it had been ordained they would arrive last. Mother Nature had informed Alice that Sophie Narey's arrival would be the sign that the last human being left in Great Britain had arrived. Now that Sophie was present, Alice had her scribe, and so, could begin the New History of the World through the eyes of an unspoiled human with no allegiances to anyone. Alice Winters-Chambers and Sophie Narey were now the Atkinson and Dewhirst of the Plane of Existence, with one main difference...Alice and Sophie were about Life, not Death.

Alice and Sophie had adjourned to a quiet spot to get to know each other when Alice noticed Delphinium sitting upon Sophie's shoulder.

"Who do we have here?"

"This is Delphinium...she is my friend. It is her job to keep me safe, and to make sure my pen's ink doesn't run dry."

"It's a pleasure to meet one of Mother's creatures from her realm. I look forward to the day when more of you arrive," smiled Alice.

"It is a pleasure to meet the one Mother chose to carry on in her stead," said Delphinium, as she bowed her head.

"The pleasure is mine...it's wonderful to still be alive...but to be able to witness all that I have, and see all the things to come is truly an honour, indeed," said Alice.

The three females smiled and chatted over the next hour, and plans as to how they would work together were made.

The rest of Sophie's friends mingled with the people in the commune, perfectly at ease with what they were about to begin.

When they all had eaten, drank, and refreshed themselves, they simply joined in with the work as if they had been builders for years. Back in the shelter, Michael, Jamie, Freddie, and Jack were going over in fine detail the plans that had been redrawn by Julia Naylor...in particular, the ones for the new kitchen and dining area.

The kitchen would be large enough to accommodate up to 10 people working there at any one time, which was more than enough to satisfy the needs of the people they had living in the commune. The seating within the dining area would hold half the commune at each sitting, so the meals would be staggered, and the kitchen crew would work full-time, should Alice find 10 residents willing to undertake such a task.

Whilst going over the plans for the buildings, Jamie stumbled upon two new drawings; these were the last two plans that Julia Naylor drew after completing the revised log cabins. These schematics that Julia had introduced included plans for two mills...a windmill, and more importantly, a watermill. Jamie stared at the plans; he knew the windmill was a good way off in the future, as for a while, there would be no grain to grind...however, he was also aware that a watermill would be the single biggest development for the commune. Most of all, he was the only one who could fashion the parts that Julia had no knowledge of – the all-important gearing.

Jamie had taken stock of certain items in the safety shelter...items which, at first glance, looked strange – because they appeared to be parts of machinery, such as a large circular saw blade, etc. He revisited the shelter's storeroom to evaluate what he had to work with. Mother Nature seemed to know more about historical machinery than Jamie did, as everything he needed for the interior of his watermill was now at his disposal, right in front of him.

A smile came to his face, as he recalled his second trip in Mother Nature's time machine vortex. Thanks to Mother Nature, and her ability to send people back in time, he was about to use the ancient knowledge he'd learned centuries before he was born.

Jamie and his sister had returned from their Switch in Time, sending another pair of siblings from Victorian England back to their own era. Once back in the 21st century, a brief respite ensued, then whilst his sister began the fundamental stages of preparing for the Apocalypse, he was sent even further back by the Goddess to discover the value of wind and water power. Upon his return, he couldn't really understand why this particular episode of time travel had occurred. His interest lay in steam...he had already visited the Industrial Revolution, and indeed worked in a factory that produced steam locomotives whilst setting up a new life for his ancestor John Watson, who later became John Winters, a very talented steam engineer. Pondering upon his time travels brought Laura Dinsdale back to mind. He wondered how long he would have to wait to kiss her lips once again.

You will be reunited as soon as your watermill is complete, said the Goddess' voice in his head.

The completed watermill had now totally taken over Jamie's plans. Only now had it all become clear as to why he had learned this ancient technology. It would be some time before steam could be produced, and power would be needed before then...but not the kind of energy Jack Howard could invoke. The commune needed physical power to generate new things – Jamie Winters had been gifted the knowledge of how this was accomplished, and he was going to use that gift. He left the storeroom with a spring in his step, a smile on his face, and the promise of love in his heart.

John Smith and Tom Harper were having a quiet moment together when Tom said, "There are a few things we need to discuss, John."

"Ask me whatever you want – I will answer you truthfully," said John.

"You appear to be more than you seem...quite a lot more, in fact," said Tom.

"Yes, I am...but I am also the accountant you met and fell in love with, and although accountants are not needed in this New World, I am still the same man you met. There is much to discover in this New World...wondrous sights, sounds, and all it has to offer will be at your fingertips. As I once said to my friend and your boss Gavin Jackson, scientific thinking will get in the way of who you now are."

"I understand that. I have a basic idea of who I think you are, but I need to hear it from you."

"Are you ready to hear this? Are you capable of comprehending what I say to you?"

"I need to hear it from you, John. I know that there is a different you...one who is powerful and otherworldly. I need to know who that person is," pressed Tom.

"I am the fourth horse-rider of the Apocalypse...Death...the Grim Reaper. I have just laid waste to almost 7,000,000,000 people. You asked me, and I have answered. Now, you must ask yourself – firstly, do you believe me, and secondly, can you live with that? I am an Immortal being...my appearance will never change. I will never grow old, and in 50 years' time, I will begin reaping the souls of all the people you see around you – including you. As you can see, there is an awful lot more to me than you knew...maybe too much more."

Tom lowered his head as he tried to take in what his lover had just told him, but try as he might, he could not grapple with the intensity of what John had just said. All that had happened over the past month had shown that there was so much more to the world than his scientific brain understood. The creatures he had seen backed up what John had just revealed. *Of all things though, why did he have to be the Grim Reaper, with the blood of the world on his hands?* thought Tom.

"The blood of the world is not on my hands — for that to be true I would need a conscience. Death has no conscience...nor does it have pity, or a sense of shame. When someone's time is up, I transfer the soul of that person to another about to be born. I achieve this by taking the life of the person whose life number has run its course, with no emotion or any feelings whatsoever. In the ethereal world, I am Death...nothing more nothing less. On the Plane of Existence, I am John Smith...a shy, gay man. Until your demise, he is the only part of me that you will know. I will leave you alone now, so you can come to terms with what I have told you, and decide upon what you want — or may not want — to do."

John Smith slowly stood and walked away, leaving Tom Harper sitting with his head in his hands, tears rolling down his cheeks. In his heart, John Smith knew his short love affair with Tom Harper was over. He saw no further reason for lingering, and decided there and then to return to the old Tudor building within the Other Realm and sit out the 50 years with Mr. Braithwaite and his companions. John Smith walked out of the commune, never to return.

Sarah and Gavin both felt John Smith leaving the Plane of Existence, and a realisation began to form in their minds that maybe that was the right thing to do...interference from Immortals was probably not a good idea. If humans grew to rely upon the things Immortals could do, they may not try as hard to accomplish tasks themselves. As Gavin and Sarah's thoughts passed to and from each other, another thought entered their heads.

You are wise to think this way...the three of you could have made a tremendous difference, but that difference may have made things too easy for the ones left to start again...as with the clearing and sawing of the trees. I did not interfere when you decided to return to the Plane of Existence, but I'm glad you are now thinking this way. Come and stay with me in the Realm of

Nature...spend the next 50 years making love, and living a normal life. There is no need for Warriors until it is time for you to return to the Other Realm.

The voice of Mother Nature dissipated from their collective minds and the decision was made to take Mother Nature up on her offer, following John's example and putting the Plane of Existence to their backs. Without ceremony, the Earth Mother Warrior and the Sentinel arrived in the Realm of Nature.

Back in the commune, Sophie Narey wondered by and asked Alice Winters-Chambers if her friend Slabgirl had arrived.

"Slabgirl?"

"Sorry...her name is Sarah...she is married to Gavin Jackson."

Alice thought for a moment, then said, "There is nobody in the commune with the name Sarah, Gavin, or Jackson, I'm afraid..."

"I don't know why, but I thought – I mean, I hoped – they might be here," said Sophie disappointedly.

Within the Realm of Nature – and more specifically, in the Valley of the Extinct – Mia, the Unicorn Queen, was making her morning rounds to check on her beloved yet extinct animals. She was the protector of the Animal Communication Charm – a charm so powerful that once initiated, any species could speak fluently to another. Her full title was Mia – Queen of the Enchanted Animals...but everyone knew her as Mia, the Unicorn Queen, for it was no secret who her favourite beasts were. Although she loved all animals, there was a special place in her heart for the herd of unicorns within the valley; this was because she had the blood of the unicorn surging through her veins.

She saw the herd of unicorns galloping through the morning mist towards the Great Lake. She instantly morphed into her unicorn self and chased after the herd, catching up with them just as they reached the lake, and all were pleased to see her. A majestic stallion standing 20 hands tall joined her as she drank from the lake. Both Mia and he turned into human form as they greeted one another.

"My Queen...you honour us with your presence! do you bring news of Juliantrium?" asked Gustaf, the leader of the herd.

"Juliantrium is well...she is resting after her Apocalyptic duties...but Juliantrium is not the reason I am here. I bring news of great importance...Gustaf, I will be taking you and the herd back onto the Plane of Existence, as part of Mother's regeneration of the planet," smiled Mia.

"We had heard rumours, but didn't dare believe! Is what you say true? If it is, this is a most auspicious day, and must be celebrated!" enthused Gustaf.

"The words I speak are the words of Mother Nature," assured Mia.

"Then I must relay this message to the others! Will you join us in our celebrations?" invited Gustaf.

"Other species await this wonderful news, as you are not the only ones to return. All Mother's creatures who are now extinct – but not through evolution – are to return, and I am the lucky one to deliver such glad tidings," said Mia.

Gustaf and Mia, having reverted back to their unicorn guise lowered their heads until their horns touched. He then rose onto his hind legs, Mia mirroring his actions, as they touched hooves in the classic unicorn farewell. Gustaf sped away to the herd to deliver his exciting news, whilst Mia left to visit the Centaurs.

The Centaurs were expecting Mia, as their leader had already heard from Mother Nature of her plan for their return to the Plane of Existence. Although they knew, they displayed the same exuberance for the news. Mia was greatly enjoying this time, as she readied the animals Mother Nature had placed under her care. She had many different species to inform of the plan, but she had a generous amount of time to achieve her goal. The time afforded her was such that because apart from getting the humans to live without hunting, Mother Nature also knew she needed it to ready all of the animals. Some of these animals – not unlike the unicorns and the centaurs were scared of humans, and would be frightened at the thought of returning. Mother Nature knew she could trust Mia to convince these less-dominant creatures they would be perfectly safe, and could enjoy their life once more upon the Plane of Existence. Twelve moons would wax and wane during the time of preparation, and the first of those moons was full and shining brightly in the clear sky above the Valley of the Extinct.

Back on the Plane of Existence, that same moon's pale face shone down from the beautiful starlit sky. Humanity's first month on the New Earth was complete – and what a month it had been. Alice Winters-Chambers had her full complement of people within the commune, all of whom had settled in and were perfectly at ease with their new life. The clearing of the entire area for the dwellings had been completed, and the building work was well underway. Seven log cabins had been erected, five of which had been fitted with furniture. This furniture had been fashioned using materials from the shelter, but soon all the materials needed would be produced with what Nature provided in the forest surrounding the commune.

The knowledge of how to build furniture – such as beds, tables and chairs, wardrobes, and soft furnishings – had been placed firmly within the memory of two people within the commune... Keith Johnson, a carpenter with knowledge of ancient weaving looms and spinning wheels, and Diane Sanders, a crafter with knowledge of spinning and weaving. Diane had arrived with the Southern group of travellers, whilst Keith was one of the lucky survivors from Leeds. Diane and Keith teamed up in the second week as the first two of the dwellings neared completion, and now shared a makeshift workroom within the shelter, in keeping with the bundle of plans drawn up by Julia Naylor, which bore an illustration of a mutual space for the commune's carpenter and tailor. Not only had Keith and Diane struck up a fantastic work relationship, they enjoyed each other's company so much they were the first to register with Alice for a shared dwelling.

Alice had placed upon the shelter's wall a whiteboard and marker pen for people to register who they wanted to live with. She'd thought it might take a good while for people to find a partner, but that concern was dealt with the night Tamara and Atkinson began a new life with the God that now grew within her womb. No favouritism would be shown when it came to handing out the dwellings.

A meeting had been held with the entire group of survivors, and a unanimous decision had been made that everyone should move in en mass, when the last log cabin was finished. This decision made things a lot simpler for the carpenter and crafter, as they could make patterns first, then produce the required quantity of each piece of furniture. If everything went to plan, they would finish the final piece when the last log cabin neared its completion.

Within the shelter, Keith and Diane were hard at work. Keith was making simple beds, whilst Diane fashioned mattresses. For the entire time it would take to make the mattresses, seat covers, and the soft furnishings needed, Diane would have use of a sewing machine. In all, she had four machines – none of which used electricity – they were all controlled by a foot pedal, with a belt driving the needle. She had an extensive sewing kit, with a stack of needles which would last many lifetimes, and an abundance of different threads. Keith Johnson was gifted a toolbox filled with hand tools, and equipment to keep them sharp. He also had an array of medieval tools, such as axes and adzes for cutting and shaping large pieces of wood, and flails for splitting down the grain to slice the wood in two. However, most of his tools were the usual carpenter's wares, such as planes, hammers, chisels, and saws.

Mother Nature had made sure these two people were well-equipped, as it would be some time before the tools they needed could be made by the commune. As far as Goddess was concerned, this wasn't about sending people back to see if they could live like the ancients...this was about starting again, and giving Humanity a little push in the right direction.

This was the reason why, at the outset, if anything was needed, it was supplied. Mother Nature had given her children that survived the desire to learn new things, and the knowledge that one day they would have to make their own tools as they adapted to their new lives in the commune. Once they did, they truly would be self-sufficient, and empowered.

In the darkness by the riverbed, Alice was taking a break in the cool shadows for what seemed the first time in many days. She sensed a presence behind her, and a warm feeling came over her.

"Alice, my child...how well your brood is doing! I am very pleased with what I am witnessing. This is how I envisaged Humanity...all happily working together, and playing together. You are proving to be an excellent choice, as you are leading by example, and every time I see you, you have a smile on your face. That smile passes throughout the commune, and is returned manyfold. Your people love you, and you them...I could not ask for anything more. Now that you have everything running smoothly, it is time for you to pass my words on to the rest of my children throughout the planet, and for Sophie to take note of everything that transpires."

"How do I make the journey, Mother?"

"All you have to do is simply think 'take me to the next commune', and I will send you and Sophie there."

"When do you want me to leave?" asked Alice.

"The moon begins to wane tomorrow, so that seems a good day to begin your journey."

"We will be ready, Mother," said Alice, bowing her head.

The conversation drew to a close, and the Goddess of Nature disappeared back to her realm. Alice returned from the river strolling through the trees, with a happy feeling in her heart, and a smile on her beautiful face, knowing that everything was on schedule and to Mother Nature's liking. She looked forward to the oncoming days, as her travels around the world were about to begin. As soon as she arrived back at the commune, she gently took Sophie Narey to one side, and said, "Tomorrow, we leave here, and journey around the world. It is of the upmost importance that you capture everything in your book...not just for my personal use, but to ensure history is recorded properly. I'm looking forward to travelling with you...how do you feel about it?"

"I can't wait! I have been looking forward to this! We shall have Delphinium with us, so we know we will be safe," said Sophie.

Chapter Seven

Morning broke on the first day of the second month. It was time for Alice and Sophie to leave for their journey of discovery, to see how the rest of the world was coping with their new lives. Freddie Chambers gave his wife a kiss, then embraced her.

"I will be back before you know it," smiled Alice.

"You will be missed – and not only by me. I hope all goes well, and Mother Nature brings you back to me soon," said Freddie.

Alice nodded and said, "This day was always going to happen. Now it is here, we can get this job done, and return to our lives of rebuilding. I will be back before the waning moon has waxed once more."

"I have more than enough to do to keep me distracted while you are gone," said Freddie Chambers.

Alice and Freddie kissed once more, and then parted. Alice walked over to Sophie, took hold of her hand, and in thought, connected to Mother Nature. Both girls felt a tingling sensation within their bodies, then disappeared – reappearing in what used to be Ireland. The shelter in Ireland was the one Alice was worried about, because she had the knowledge that Ireland took the full blast of Aquallia's apocalyptical waves from the Atlantic Ocean. Finding that there were survivours on the Green Isle was a simply fantastic start for Alice's travels.

The Irish survivors saw Alice, and immediately walked over to her. All fifty people were still alive, and safe. There were no cave-dwelling survivors as all caves had been placed on the mainland of the British Isles, and anyone from Ireland, like Sophie Narey, had been placed there. As in Leeds, trees had been cleared near a rapidly-flowing river, and log cabins were being erected. As there were fewer people in the Irish contingent, the cleared area was smaller, but it seemed that the designs used back in Leeds were also somehow being used here. Alice glanced at Sophie, who was industriously writing down her observations. Delphinium, noticing her confusion skipped from Sophie's shoulder to Alice's and whispered in her ear, "Everything you do in Leeds is mirrored all over the world...that is why Mother Nature is with you, and there are so many others like me...with you, we're making sure you don't make mistakes."

"That's reassuring to know," said Alice, as she greeted her new Irish friends.

The good people of Ireland as was all knew of Alice...the winged creatures had foretold of her coming, and they were eager to impress her. As they took Alice by the hand and showed her around the work they had already accomplished, she was impressed – or, rather, Mother Nature, through Alice's eyes, was impressed – with all they had achieved. Alice was led inside one of the finished log cabins, and it pleased her that all the furniture and soft furnishings were of the same design as her own in Leeds. One thing the Irish were ahead on was tea-making. Amongst them was a botanist, not part of the general workforce, who had been assigned to finding and tending to edible plants. No time was wasted by her doing mundane tasks in her tireless pursuit of precuring new foods.

Sally Carpenter's forays into the woods surrounding the commune had led to many useful discoveries – one of which was that tea plants now grew in the Northern Hemisphere, in quite an abundance. Within the first week since been selected as the commune's botanist, Sally discovered lemons flourishing freely. She found this hard to take in at first, but as hers and everyone else's memory of the past faded, the knowledge that lemons and tea did not grow in their part of the world faded with it. Alice listened intently as Sally Carpenter told her of the discoveries she had made. Whilst Sally was talking, Alice – through thought transference – entered the mind of Kareem Farmer. Kareem was the person chosen as the botanist back in Leeds.

Meanwhile back In Leeds, Kareem was busy sawing logs when the thought entered his mind to go see Jasmine Lester, which he immediately did.

"Ah...Kareem! I was about to come and see you!" said Jasmine upon his arrival.

"Well, I am here – what would you like to see me about? You already have the plans for the buildings..." answered the one-time architect.

"It isn't your architectural skills that we need right now – you are a botanist, and as such, your duties have changed. We would appreciate it if you would accept this role, and begin seeking out different foods the community to eat. I have it on good authority that tea now grows in this part of the world," said Jasmine.

Kareem raised an eyebrow, as he knew that tea could not grow in their part of the world...or, rather, he used to know that. He accepted what Jasmine had just told him, and the challenge she had set.

"When would you like me to start?" asked Kareem.

"You just have," said Jasmine, as the broadest smile illuminated her beautiful face.

Kareem Farmer was filled with joy and excitement as he ran to find his friend Wendy Walters to tell her the good news. Unbeknownst to him, as he reached her she'd already been made privy to the news, but that didn't spoil the excitement of the moment as they embraced.

"Isn't this wonderful?" enthused Wendy.

"I can pick up where I left off! Surely now, people will love my ideas of all-natural products containing no chemicals which could hurt the bees or the crops," said a thrilled Kareem.

Back in what used to be Ireland, Alice asked who was actually in charge of the commune. The reason for this was because she'd had no contact at all from that particular shelter, and had assumed it to be lost to the Apocalypse after Sophie had related her account of what had happened there. Nobody could be more pleased than she that the commune had survived. A young man stood and said, "We have no leader...we all just seemed to know what to do."

"In that case, I must commend you all on what you have achieved so far. How close are we to the river?" asked Alice.

"It's just through here— if you would like to follow me I will show you," invited Sally.

"Lead on," said Alice.

Sophie Narey continued recording all that was taking place in her journal, whilst being accompanied by Delphinium.

"Have you noticed nobody seems to find it strange that I have a fairy on my shoulder?" asked Sophie.

"That is because the memory of beings like me not existing has erased from their collective consciousness," replied Delphinium.

At the river's edge, Alice, Sophie, Delphinium, and Sally were joined by Grace Murphy. Grace was a carpenter, and had been drawn from her work within the commune to where Alice and Sally stood.

"Who do we have here?" smiled Alice.

"This is Grace...she is the clever person that showed us how to put our log cabins together," said Sally.

"I am very pleased to meet you...we have several people back on the mainland with knowledge of wood crafting...if you take my hand, Grace, I will link you with one of them," invited Alice.

Grace Murphy looked at Sally, and Sally nodded her head. Grace then grasped Alice's hand, and a warm feeling of friendship filled her entire being. Back in Leeds, Jamie Winters felt the same sensation, as his mind – through his sister's own – was aligned with his Irish counterpart. Grace Murphy's eyes opened wide as she saw an image of a watermill where they now stood, and although she'd never built such a thing, she now possessed the knowledge of how to do so. She let go of Alice's hand, ran a few yards towards the water, and exclaimed with excitement, "I am going to build a watermill – right here where we stand! All the wood I need is around us, and the working parts are inside the shelter!"

"There is nothing like that in the shelter..." a confused Sally shook her head.

Alice took Sally's hand, and said, "I think you will find that now, there probably is."

Grace took off for the shelter, and true enough, all the gearing, belts, wheels, shafts, and everything to fit them into place was there waiting for her.

Whilst the thought transference between the botanists and builders was taking place, Mother Nature linked every pair like them on the planet to their respective counterparts, and the knowledge of what had been achieved – and the what could be achieved – was shared worldwide.

Alice, Sophie, and Sally caught up with Grace at the shelter. She was busy taking inventory of all the working parts.

"As soon as we have completed the log cabins built, I'm building a watermill," said a very excited Grace.

"Then, our work here is done. You all are doing remarkably well...Keep up the good work! If anyone needs to ask a question, just think my name – Alice Winters-Chambers – and in thought, I will answer."

Sophie Narey closed her journal as she took Alice's hand, and the two women set off for what used to be Europe, stopping first in France.

Back in Leeds, Kareem Farmer began his new life as a botanist, as he placed a collecting bag over his shoulder, and strapped on a utility belt. This useful belt contained a trowel, a pair of secateurs, a container full of sample bags, and a packed lunch, and was now fully ready as he buckled it into position. He bid farewell to his friends, and walked into the woods. A happy man was he as he whistled the song he had sung with the others he journeyed from Wales with. Kareem had several plants in mind that he wanted to find...one of them was tea, and another, cotton.

As he delved deeper into the woods, he noticed the surrounding atmosphere of the place changing. He likened this to entering the old Canal Gardens in a place called Roundhay park that he once visited as a child. Within those gardens, there was a large greenhouse-type building known as Tropical World. Inside that building, the temperature was set to resemble the Amazon Rain Forest. Where he now stood, he had the same feeling as he'd felt the day he visited that popular tourist attraction back in his youth.

All knowledge of tropical weather being reserved for certain regions had been removed from the collective conscience. These arrangements made by Mother Nature whilst international travel was unavailable made it possible for all her survivors to thrive and develop at the same rate. This system would eventually revert back to how the climate of the world should be when New Humanity Reaches 2,000 years. By that time, Mother Nature's enlightened Homo Supremus will have far surpassed its predecessors, which were – on all fronts – regressing back to Homo Erectus.

A host of magnificent butterflies – all of which were larger than his hand – greeted Kareem. He noticed extremely large grubs in the trees, and on the ground. He eagerly began collecting the grubs, as he knew they were a brilliant form of protein...but as he picked up the first one to place it in his bag, he stopped and said out loud, "Mother Nature...may I use these creatures as a food source?"

Kareem suddenly felt a presence – a feeling he was no longer alone. He turned around, and standing there was the Goddess herself. Kareem fell to his knees at the sight of her.

"Rise, my child," said Mother Nature.

Kareem did as he was bid. Mother Nature spoke again. "Kareem Farmer, you have been tasked to find food for my commune. Everything is at your disposal for that purpose...but take only what you need. There is no need for hoarding food – if you abide by that simple law, you need never fear about utilising the food chain...just remember, animals are no longer part of the your food chain. They may hunt each other when they return to the forests, but they will not hunt humans. This is your opportunity, as the gifted botanist that you are, to break away from eating meat. You will find the rewards the animals give you far outweigh the benefits of eating their flesh. I hope this has answered your question, and I do appreciate you asking my permission. Kareem Farmer, now go in peace, and feed your people."

With those words, Mother Nature disappeared, and a startled but happy botanist carried on collecting his bugs.

Within the commune, the building carried on at a good pace. Whilst Alice was away, Jasmine Lester – with help of Wendy Walters and Simone Baudelaire – ran the commune as promised. There was no slowing down...everyone carried on as if Alice was still there, because in their collective conscience, she was. Jasmine knew if she needed Alice, she was only a thought away. This reassurance was all she needed to perform her work well. Jasmine's daughter Mina, as well as being a brilliant motivator, was proving to be a good worker, too – as she and three others lifted a log into place at the near-completion of yet another log cabin. Smiling and laughter were the order of the day for the workforce, as every single person within the commune was learning new skills, and finding new boundaries that they could stretch themselves beyond. There was definitely a feeling that they were building their future...not just log cabins.

The construction of the cabins in Leeds was mirrored around the planet at every large commune, and each community with 50 people was at the exact same stage as their Irish contingent. Alice Winters-Chambers had now been travelling for over two weeks, and had visited many countries. Each time, she passed on all she had learned from every different commune to each new community that she discovered. Everything she learned she also passed back to Jasmine Lester through thought, then Jasmine shared these teachings to everyone in her commune. A collective knowledge from around the world was being passed to every part of the world, and every commune grew with this knowledge, and thrived.

Alice and Sophie Neary had seen many places during their time away from the commune in Leeds, and had learned and taught many things. Alice was watching Sophie, who was busy writing in her journal about the people they had met in Japan – or rather what used to be Japan, when something caught her eye. At first, Alice thought it was some kind of animal. It was unkempt, with very long, tatty white hair...it was naked, and its posture resembled that of the female human. For some reason, it lingered outside the camp...so Alice walked over to it and beckoned it towards her. The creature tried to walk towards Alice, but it was as if an invisible force was keeping it out of the commune. Alice exited the commune, and strode up to the beast. It was crouched down, and lowered its head as Alice approached.

"Who are you? why don't you come inside," asked Alice with concern.

Alice could now see that this was an old woman...a very old woman. She had no teeth, and her eyes were blind. Her ribcage could be seen clearly through her paper-thin skin. She was not the new colour of Humanity...underneath the grime, she was clearly Caucasian. The woman tried to answer Alice, but her croaked words were incoherent. She lifted her hand up to Alice; her fingernails were so long, that they curled and spiraled into her palms. It was becoming clear that this ancient human had not used her hands – or her mouth – for a very long time.

Alice's heart contracted with pity for this woman and she called upon Mother Nature to find out who she was.

*This beast of a woman had many vices...she was truly one of the worst people on the planet. She was a murderous, treacherous person – and needed to be taught a lesson. Paladin decided she would walk the Earth, until she found Absolution from the Reapers...*answered Mother Nature in thought.

"How long has she been like this?" asked Alice agog.

She has been in this state since before the Apocalypse.

"She has been wandering the Earth for over 300 years?"

It was decreed that she would do so.

"We are now living in a time of Absolution...I see no purpose in this woman continuing her penitence. These people do not need to see this abomination as they begin their new lives. With the greatest respect, Mother, I urge you to put an end to this existence," begged Alice.

Within the Realm of Nature, Mother Nature pondered upon what Alice had just asked her. She saw how wise Alice had become, and made contact with Paladin.

Mother...how can I be of service?

The being you cast adrift after your visit to Japan – Alice has come upon her. She has asked me if Absolution can be granted as she doesn't want her people to have to witness such a despicable relic from the past. Alice has a good heart, and was only thinking of others when she has requested this of me. You are the one who cast this person adrift...it is for you to decide whether she should be passed to the Reapers or continue her ordeal.

It was not my intention for this woman to be seen by the New Civilization, and to this end I agree with Alice. I remove her banishment; will you let the Reaper know or should I, great Mother?

You have become wise in your judgement, Paladin – I applaud that, and am very proud of you. You can inform the Reaper – but not Atkinson – inform Smith and have him deal with it.

Your will is my command, Mother...I will deal with it forthwith.

Mother Nature materialised in front of Alice Winters-Chambers and the old woman. She gazed upon Old Humanity with distaste, then turned her glance to Alice and said, "You are proving yourself to be wise, Alice...and, proving me correct in choosing you. Your wish will be fulfilled, and this wretched beast will be slain."

As Mother Nature and Alice were talking, John Smith entered the Realm of Death for the first time in months. He breathed in the air, and reacquainted himself with his old domain. A grin came to his face as a single mortal cord lowered itself from the ceiling. He grasped the cord but instead of slicing through it, he placed little cuts all the way down its length. The old woman screamed in agony every time the Reaper gouged a scar in the cord. Alice looked away, but Mother Nature – knowing the many evils that this woman had performed – watched with no feeling of remorse.

John Smith put a loop in the tattered cord, then sliced it in two. The woman – who before the Apocalypse dealt in human trafficking, illegal whaling, prostitution, fraud, and every other vice she could put her grubby hands to – unceremoniously died in front of them.

Alice asked Mother Nature what she should do with her remains.

"Leave her to rot," said Mother Nature, as she disappeared back to her own realm.

Sophie Narey recorded everything that was said by entering it into her journal. If proof was needed that Mother Nature could be as ruthless as she was kind, the Apocalypse had shown it, and what had just taken place asserted the fact. She was a loving Goddess...as long as you didn't cross her.

Chapter Eight

It was a special day in Leeds, as it was all over the world. Alice Winters-Chambers had been back in her commune for some time, and had been looking forward to this day. It was the topping out ceremony of the last log cabin. The living and dining components of the commune were complete. 150 dwellings, a kitchen, and a dining room had all been finished within the first year.

The time had come for everyone to move in en mass, and there was a festive atmosphere, as all had looked forward to this day. Another event about to take place was the imminent arrival of the babies conceived nine months prior to that day, when Atkinson and Tamara – with the help of Mother Nature and Pan – began the rebirth of Humanity.

Amongst the happy throng of people enjoying the day was Erin Adams. As the ex-librarian was enjoying the festivities, she suddenly felt a warm sensation in her lower body. Erin then realised she was drenched with fluid, and her waters had broken. She let out a yelp as the shock of what was about to happen took hold of her. Almost instantly, Viktoria and Linda Harper ran to her assistance. The two women escorted Erin into one of the finished log cabins, and laid her on the bed.

Viktoria and Linda had been gifted the knowledge of midwifery by Mother Nature in preparation of this unprecedented event about to take place, which would begin with Erin Adams, and carry on throughout the following week.

John Smith entered the Realm of Death to achieve the exact opposite of what he helped Atkinson carry out during the Apocalypse. He had a plethora of mortal cords awaiting attachment to a new life. As Erin's cervix dilated to 10 centimeters, the Reaper connected the mortal cord – accompanied by the usual flash of light – to the unborn infant, and the first human to be born in the New Era was on his way. Within the hour Erin's partner came outside, and lifted the baby high for everyone to see. The entire mass of people, almost half of them pregnant themselves, cheered and celebrated whilst making ready for their own deliveries.

Freddie Chambers grew concerned, and said to his wife, Alice, "You've been pregnant longer than Erin…when will our twins be born?"

"Our babies are different to the rest, Freddie – they will take longer to gestate."

"Why?" mused a befuddled Freddie.

"Because our babies shall carry on our work long into the future. The numerous babies being born now are to restock Humanity; our babies will be born to guide the new generation of people when we no longer can. All I know is there is still a ways to go before I deliver them to you. The truth is, I don't know how long I will be pregnant…only Mother Nature knows that," said Alice.

"That's ok, then…as they are special, Mother Nature won't let anything happen to them. She most certainly knows what she is doing," smiled Freddie Chambers, as he gave his wife a loving kiss.

Viktoria and Linda were soon called to someone else's aid to assist in the delivery of the next child being born. As this was happening, everyone else in the commune began to enter their log cabins. Whilst settling into their new abodes, each New World parent readied their home for the new arrival. Not everyone within the commune was expecting a new delivery, however, and there were exceptions.

Jack Howard was asexual. Viktoria and Linda Harper were lesbians. Tom Harper and Steve Bingham were gay, and Sophie Narey – although of straight sexual orientation, and in her child-bearing years – was deemed by Mother Nature as too busy for motherhood at this moment in time...however, in Sophie's case, that was a temporary situation.

As John Smith had walked out of Tom Harper's life, the knowledge of ever knowing the Reaper left with him, too. This gave Tom Harper a trouble-free mind, so he could start again. During the construction of the log cabins, Tom Harper and Steve Bingham had grown quite close...so much so that they now shared a cabin, one that they hoped would be theirs together for the rest of their lives.

Mother Nature looked upon Tom and Steve, and Linda and Viktoria, and decided they should not remain childless because of a natural phenomenon. Being Gay or Lesbian was not a life choice...they had not actively chosen to remain childless. The Goddess decided there and then that after she brought the animals back to the Plane of Existence, she would address the matter. The only person out of this loop was Jack Howard...but Mother Nature knew his work in her New World was just as important as the rebuilding of her enlightened species of Humankind.

One of the reasons for Jack Howard's new role now came into play, as he visited each dwelling and set the lighting in each room to how the individual couple wanted it. It took a full day to accomplish that task, and by the time he had finished the last dwelling, a further eleven babies had been born and many more were on their way.

Diane Sanders had moved onto making baby essentials after she'd finished the soft furnishings for Keith Johnson's wooden furniture. She had spent the previous week sewing nappies, and whilst Jack Howard had been filling the rooms with light, Diane had visited each abode leaving 20 nappies for every couple. Along with the nappies, she had also fashioned each of the newborn babies a set of clothes which would fit them until they were three months old. Diane had a goodly amount of cloth, but it wouldn't last forever. With this in mind, Keith had begun working on making a spinning wheel from which she could spin and thread the wool of sheep once they returned.

Plans were also pinned to Keith's wall for a foot-pedal-controlled weaving loom. This piece of equipment would need working parts...the parts as yet weren't available to them, but the Goddess of Nature had already placed what Keith needed into his store room. The drawing of said loom had also caught the attention of Jamie Winters, who had become great friends with Keith. Jamie called in to see Keith as he'd promised the day before, to help him with a new machine the carpenter had built.

All the wooden parts for the spinning wheel had been cut and roughly shaped with the hand tools at Keith's disposal. However, the actual spokes for the wheel itself needed to be made. Keith had fashioned a crude – but very clever – lathe to complete this work, but it required two people to operate it. Keith would be the one handling the chisel, and Jamie would provide the power.

The lathe was a simple affair, consisting of two large half-logs cut to lengths of 5 feet – 18 inches of which had been buried in the ground for stability. The two 3 ½ feet lengths protruding out of the ground were set 3 feet apart. Through the top of the left upright, a 2 inch hole had been drilled, and through this hole, a piece of wood pointed at the end was driven in and fixed into place. On the right upright was a 3 inch hole which the wood about to be turned would fit through; the end of each piece of wood to be shaped had been rounded off to fit through this hole.

On the outside of the upright, connected to the piece of wood about to be turned was a 6 x 2 inch disc. The wood about to be shaped was keyed into the disc so there would be no slipping. A belt to a larger disc of the same thickness then connected the turning and power discs. A handle had been attached to the larger disc, and Jamie would turn the handle as fast as he could to power the spindle as Keith shaped the wood with his chisel.

The two friends were ready to try the first machine to be built in the Industrial Revolution of the New Age. Keith positioned the piece of wood between the two uprights, placing one side through the power end of the apparatus, then the other end of the wood to the pointed piece attached to the opposite upright. The point fitted snugly into the hole at the end of the wood that Keith had prepared. Just on the inside of the powered upright, there had been a hole drilled through the wood to be shaped. Through this, a small length of wood had been slipped to prevent the turning piece retracting.

Jamie knew, as did Keith, that this arrangement would not be suitable when the watermill was complete, and many adaptations would have to be made for when the workshop recieved proper power. For this purpose, however, the new lathe would function well.

"Are you ready?" asked Keith.

Jamie nodded, then began to turn the wheel. The wood held between the two posts began to turn as Keith placed the simple chisel rest before the now-spinning piece of wood. The sharp, heavy-duty chisel soon had shaved the corners down to something resembling a spoke. He then Grasped a length of sandpaper, and sanded the spoke to a nice, smooth finish as the first of the six spokes was completed. Keith looked happy with his new spoke, and his reinvention of the lathe had worked perfectly. Jamie, however, realised it was definitely time to start building the mill, because he was wet through with sweat after half an hour of handle-turning, which had produced just one wheel spoke...albeit a very nice one.

The two men stuck to their task, and after a lot of anguish and sweat, the six spokes were finished and ready to fit into the wheel's centre. When that task was complete, it was time to fix the other ends of the spokes to the six separate pieces of shaped wood which would form the outer rim of the wheel. All of these fit perfectly into place as Keith's mastery of woodwork clearly shone through. He tapped each piece gently into place upon the spokes, so that it looked like a proper wheel. Keith put a tourniquet around the outside of the wheel, placing a length of wood between it and the wheel. He then twisted the length of wood, to tighten the rope around the wheel. The wood creaked as all the separate parts were forced together. Next, he drilled six holes through the rim, with matching ones though the center, also drilling through the spokes at each end. Through each centre hole, he tapped through pieces of dowel to hold everything together, repeating the action with the joints in the six pieces of the rim. Once the last dowel was in place, the wheel was finished, and the tourniquet removed.

Both men stood back and admired the work they had just completed. Keith was happy with how the wheel had turned out. In his prior way of working he would of course have used glue, but that was not an option now, so the old method of using the dowels had come into play. Jamie picked up the wheel and inspected it; a smile came to his face as he realised they had a gem of a craftsman within their community. Jamie was still smiling when he turned to look at Keith. "This is absolutely perfect...and the lathe worked brilliantly! We now know when the time comes for us to produce agricultural equipment, such as handcarts and the like, we have our man to make the wheels."

"Not just wheels! I can make ploughs, a seed drill, wooden pitchforks, rakes...I can make anything like that," enthused Keith.

"I can't tell you how much I am enjoying working with you, and looking forward to building the mills! With my knowledge of how these mills were built, and your obvious skills with woodworking, we will make a great team! I will go and let Alice know that the spinning wheel is almost complete...when should I bring her to view the finished item?"

"It will be up and running tomorrow, and I will arrange a demonstration by Diane Sanders so Alice can see it working," said Keith.

As Jamie left, Diane joined Keith.

"Hello, Keith...I see it is almost ready."

"Indeed, it is," he said, as he placed the wheel into position, and fitted the footman from the treadle plate into its attachment on the spindle of the wheel. "I think we are ready for a treadle test to see if everything works," he continued.

Diane sat on the chair Keith had made specifically for this purpose, placing her foot upon the waiting treadle plate. The toe-heel movement of her foot that she had perfected over many years of spinning as a pastime began to turn the wheel, which in turn rotated the flyer, which then spun the bobbin...everything checked out. Both Keith and Diane were happy with the result. Keith asked, "Do you have any wool to hand that you have already carded?"

"Yes I do..." said Diane, reaching into her wool caddy and picking out a couple of rolled lengths of carded wool. She attached a piece of wool to the bobbin, placing it through the hook on the side of the flyer – and then through the orifice, using a crochet needle to pull it through. She then pulled the strands of her rolled, carded fibres, twisting them around the wool attached to the bobbin. Diane began her toe-heel foot manoeuvre, and the fibres in her hand had begun to twist. She let them twist, then pushed them back along the fibres, and she was spinning wool on a working spinning wheel. Diane was so pleased with her new acquisition, she jumped up from her chair and gave Keith a loving kiss.

Keith smiled and said, "We are ready for Alice to come for a demonstration of your Saxon spinning wheel tomorrow. Now I'm going to check my plans for the weaving loom."

That statement brought an even bigger smile to Diane's lips, because she knew that once she had a weaving loom, she would be able to keep the commune in clothes far into the future.

Inside their new log cabin, Viktoria and Linda Harper were in a reflective mood as they lay in their bed.

"How do you feel?" asked Viktoria.

"What do you mean?" said Linda.

"How do you feel about all the other women becoming pregnant, and having babies?"

"Oh...I see. In all honesty, I feel strange – as if I'm missing out on something monumental. Does that make me sound selfish?" said Linda.

"Not at all! I'm feeling the same way...but there's not a great deal we can do about it, I'm afraid."

As the two girls lay on their bed, someone appeared in the room. The entire room lit up brilliantly, and then the light settled. When their eyes were accustomed to the light, they saw the figure of Mother Nature standing in before them.

"Viktoria and Linda Harper...be at ease. I am here to offer a gift...I can offer you both motherhood, should you want to accept that gift," said Mother Nature.

Both women looked at each other, then nodded. They turned to Mother Nature excitedly and said in unison, "Yes, please!"

"You haven't ventured the obvious question of 'how?' May I ask why?" said Mother Nature.

Viktoria stood and with her head lowered said, "It isn't our place to ask such a question after you saved our lives...we will do as you bid."

Mother Nature smiled and said, "I thank you for that. I'm sure you will be glad to know that the seed of life will come from me...but I ask for something in return," said the Goddess.

"State your terms and we will accept," said Linda.

"My terms are simple...I will inseminate both of you, but in return, I will take all the eggs you shall produce from now on. I do this so I may help any males in the same position as you, to gift them parenthood of their own blood. Do you agree to my terms?" asked Mother Nature.

"It would be an honour to accept what you offer," said Viktoria.

"Then come to me, my children, and accept what I give."

Viktoria and Linda walked to where Mother Nature stood...she was now as naked as they were. The Goddess placed her arms around both women, letting her hands slip down the side of both Linda and Viktoria onto their pubic areas. Mother Nature's two index fingers touched the hood of both women's clitoris, and a feeling of overwhelming pleasure shot through both their bodies. The Goddess' fingers delved deeper as she uttered an enchantment. Mother Nature then retracted her fingers and the women fell into each other's arms...both smiling...both pregnant.

Mother Nature placed her hands under the chins of both Viktoria and Linda and raised their heads. The Goddess kissed both women on the cheek, then smiled and was gone. Linda and Viktoria were left in each other's arms, with the most beautiful feeling of absolute happiness. A biological event was about to take place – one that they'd never thought possible. This event would make their lives complete – and now, they had even more to look forward to in their new lives.

The following day commenced with the usual magnificent daybreak. All within the commune began to stir...there was no need for alarm clocks, as everybody's body clock worked properly again. People slowly drifted down to the river for their morning bath. This had not only become a comfortable manner in which to behave, it was also a great time for meetings between different factions of the commune, as everyone could take part. Nursing mothers sat upon the riverbank as they fed their children, with no discrimination whatsoever. In fact, it was not unusual for a woman to advise what was going to take place that day whilst having a child suckling at her breast. As it should be, this was seen as a perfectly natural thing to do, and no one's attention was drawn to the fact that a mother was feeding her child.

One such woman was Wendy Walters, who was feeding her child whilst with a group of people discussing the construction of Jamie Winters' watermill. Although a nurse by trade, she had discovered the excitement of building during the time the log cabins were being erected, and wanted to take part in this latest project for the commune. She listened intently whilst Jamie, Michael, Jack, and Freddie were checking the area at the side of the river they had chosen for its construction.

Jamie shouted to Wendy to come and help him mark out the plot. The others returned to the commune, to sort out the materials needed for the construction. Wendy's muse had given her the confidence she needed to push herself forward when Jamie's team had been looking for people to work with. Now, here she was – in the thick of it – marking out the footings for the building.

All this was taking place whilst everyone else was still naked...so the first order of the day was to get dried and dressed. Still in the river, Alice Winters-Chambers was speaking with Keith Johnson and Diane Sanders, as she was going to their workshop straight after breakfast to see the new spinning wheel Keith had made for Diane.

"I can't remember when I was last so excited about seeing something," said Alice.

"It is a beautiful machine! I have worked with many spinning wheels, but this is by far the best one I have ever used," enthused Diane.

"My brother would say this is the first machine of his New Industrial Revolution – and he would be right! I never thought I could be as excited about machinery as my brother Jamie is, but I am! Why don't we get dried and dressed, then go to the workshop so I can see it in action?" said Alice.

All three people waded out of the river, and when dressed made their way to Keith and Diane's workroom. On entering the building, Alice excitedly looked for the spinning wheel...it was hidden under a cloth. Diane and Keith went to either side of the wheel, then Keith gave Diane the pleasure of removing the cover.

Alice gasped when she saw it...it was just like the ones she had seen in pictures. She gazed at the perfectly-made Saxon Spinning Wheel, and was very eager to see a demonstration of it working. Diane happily obliged, as she sat on the chair and carried on from where she'd left off the night before. Alice was amazed at its performance...she had never given much thought to how the bobbins of thread used for weaving were made.

"This is wonderful!" chirped Alice, clapping her hands. "Those rolls of wool you are using – is that how it comes from the sheep?"

"No, Alice...I have to wash the wool first, then I card it using these two square combs," said Diane, holding two combs up for Alice to see. "You have to comb the wool, so all of the fibres face the same way. Then, when you have run them through the combs two or three times, they are ready to roll...just like these that I'm using now," informed Diane.

"Well – I'm very impressed with your woodworking skills, Keith, and with your ability to spin yarn, Diane. I just love seeing all these things falling into place! When do you begin the weaving loom, Keith?" asked Alice.

"I have the plans and materials I need, so I will be building it alongside the watermill. In fact, it will be constructed inside the mill itself, which means I will start on it today."

"I can't believe that only 12 months into our new existence, we are at this stage – everything is going so well!" said Alice.

"Our only problem is the amount of wool I have to work with...I will need a lot of wool, and the quantity I have isn't going to be enough," worried Diane.

"As we are approaching the 12th full moon, I don't see that as a problem for much longer," said Alice, mysteriously.

"I don't understand," said a confused Diane.

"You will in the next few days," smiled Alice as she bid them both goodbye.

Chapter Nine
The Return of the Animals

Mother Nature visited Mia, the Unicorn Queen, within her domain. The Goddess of Nature was happy with how things were running in her New World, and as the 12th moon was high in the sky over the commune in Leeds, had decided it was time for her next intervention...the return her magnificent animals.

"Do you have all you require for the task at hand, Mia?" asked Mother Nature.

"I have informed all those who are returning, and they are ready Mother," said Mia.

"Then, I shall wake the people of the New World to a dawn chorus they will never forget...let us release the birds first. Await my signal, and once you have the go ahead you may begin returning the animals I saved from the planet first," said Mother Nature.

"Your wish is my command, Goddess."

Mother Nature disappeared, reappearing in the holding pen where all the winged creatures that had ever existed were roosting.

She raised her magnificent staff to the sky, and with her arms outspread, began to speak in the language only they could understand "My children of flight...hear me now! I am returning you all to the nighttime of the Earth...there, you will live in harmony with the animals known as humans."

Whistles, squawks, and all manner of bird noise filled the area...even the distinct roar of several types of dragons could be heard.

"Dawn will begin breaking in the Northern Hemisphere soon...so I release first the last to depart that world!" called Mother Nature to her children.

As she had with the arachnids and insects, the Goddess began to wave her scintillating staff in a circular motion whilst shouting out her enchanted words. The end of her staff suddenly burst into an all-encompassing blinding light.

A whole section of common birds from around the world took flight and blackened the sky, disappearing, and then reappearing on the Plane of Existence. They did not return solely to the part of the world in which they had once lived...they appeared in every country on the planet. Mother Nature had made this decision so that no one part of the world would have more than another...in other words, the wren which was common in Great Britain would sing alongside the cardinal of America, and vice versa.

Mother Nature moved from that section to the next, then was joined by Mia...in this section were the birds that were once common to the skies, but now extinct. Mother Nature looked at Mia and nodded her head. The nine-foot-tall Warrior in full regalia lifted her own staff and spoke an enchantment that awoke the long forgotten birds...not all of which could fly. Once they had been roused, Mia bowed her head and touched Mother Nature's staff with her own, then the Goddess continued her twirling motion with the staff she held, and the next section of winged creatures disappeared.

The Goddess of Nature and the Unicorn Queen then appeared in the third and final section of the holding area. In front of the two powerful females now stood the last of the beasts within the area, for this was the section containing the dragons. Mia strode up to their leader and said, "Mother Nature will now instruct you in regards to your behavior, as she is giving you another chance upon the Earth. Humans are different now, they will not hunt you...in return, you must pledge to her that you will do the same. Know this – should you harm any of Mother Nature's New Humanity, punishment for all of you will be severe and swift."

Mother Nature stepped forward, and addressed the dragons.

"I am aware that bad feelings linger between yourselves and the humans...and, as Mia has just said, they have reason to mistrust you, too. With this in mind, I am eradicating your memories of all such things. I have already removed all negative memories of dragons from the collective human mind...this means that both humans and dragons can begin with a clean slate and converse with each other, rather than fight. I will – without a second's thought – terminate the life of any dragon who defies my words."

"And what if the humans attack us? Will their fate be the same as ours?" sneered the leader of the dragons.

Mother Nature pointed her staff at the outspoken dragon, and the flash of lightning from its end terminated the dragon's existence.

"Does that make my feelings on this matter clear to everybody here – or need I demonstrate more of my wrath? I will unleash deathly fury and anger if any of you upset what I am trying to achieve...is anything of which I have just said in any way unclear? For I will cut you down in the blink of an eye should you fail me."

The silence within the dragon community spoke volumes, as the one next in line came to the fore and humbly said, "Your wish is our command...we will coexist in peace and trust with the humans."

"Much you can learn from each other in peace and tranquility. Enjoy what I bestow upon you and everything will turn out fine," advised Mother Nature.

Mia looked on as Mother Nature lifted her staff once more, and uttered her enchanted words as the dragons disappeared.

On the Plane of Existence, morning broke to the loudest-ever dawn chorus, as the returned birds sang out their pleasure at being back. Everyone came out from their log cabins to witness the event. Songbirds of every description could be heard as the beautiful music filled the air. This was the first time anyone had heard birdsong in 13 months, and all were transfixed as the harmonious sounds emanated from the trees. Alice Winters-Chambers knew this was the sign heralded the animals return.

Alice and Freddie emerged from their cabin like everyone else to enjoy the concert that the birds were performing. After a few minutes, Alice called out in a clear voice, "Prepare yourselves, everyone, we are about to have a visitor – and it is paramount that we understand everything she says to us.

There was no time for the morning dip in the river, so everyone ran back into their cabins, and dressed. As they all returned, the morning mist began to clear, and they saw – standing majestically in the middle of the commune, an Amazonian Goddess who stood at least nine feet tall.

In awe, all the people of the commune – including Alice – gathered together respectfully, and sat on the ground enraptured by the beautiful woman before them, waiting to hear her speak.

"People of this New Enlightened Age, hear me now! I am Mia – the Unicorn Queen – and what I have to say comes directly from Mother Nature, and must be adhered to without question. From this day forward, the animals shall return to coexist with you upon this planet. They hold the same rights to this planet that you hold, and are held in no greater – nor lesser – esteem than yourselves. Before the Great Cleansing, Humanity believed itself to be above the Animal Kingdom, and used Mother's animals as they saw fit, for whatever purpose they decided upon. You will find that should you behave the same way as before, Mother Nature will swiftly intervene, and stand with the animals. This is your one and only opportunity to make this co-existence work...take the opportunity, and be enlightened."

All the people within that communal area seemed stunned at the harsh words that the Goddess addressing them was using, but could still understood where she was coming from. Every single human that was listening had, at one stage of their life or another, stood up for animal rights, and was totally against battery farming. Alice rose and addressed Mia, firstly bowing her head. In her own gentle way she began to speak. "We completely understand the importance of the Animal Kingdom and will abide by any rules set out to protect their existence...on this issue, I give you my pledge."

Mia looked at Alice, and walked over to where she stood. She took hold of Alice's hands and smiled. This Animal Protection Goddess – although quite fierce – had the most beautiful smile. Alice passed the thought to her that her animals were now in a safe place.

Again, Mia spoke. "I am pleased to discover that you are all of pure heart, and I know that my animals will be safe. I now offer you a gift that Humanity has never owned...I shall bestow upon you the power of communication with the Animal Kingdom. Now, you will be able to converse...rather than consume. You will be able to learn new ways to coexist from these noble beasts of the forest. Although within the Animal Kingdom the food chain will remain intact, whilst you abide by the new ruling, human beings will no longer be a part of that chain. Any human that harms an animal will be dispatched straight to the bottom of the food chain to be consumed. Within the forest that surrounds you, there will be animals with which you're unfamiliar; some of these animals have long since left this planet through extinction. Animals that you believed only existed in mythology will roam alongside the lions, tigers, elephants, dogs, and all the other animals you know. The animals will no longer be restricted to certain continents, as every continent in the New World will be home to every species."

Upon receiving these words, there were looks of trepidation, and on some faces disbelief in what Mia was saying...especially pertaining to lions and tigers roaming the woods nearby – and what was she meaning by 'animals from mythology'.

At this point, Alice felt the need to reassure her people. "The thought of being in close proximity to such animals as lions may sound intimidating, but as Mia has just said, we are no longer food to them. More over, we can talk with them – I want you all to ponder that thought – you will be able to communicate with these animals."

Sophie Narey was writing as fast as she could, recording everything that was being said down in her journal. Delphinium who was sitting on her shoulder whispered in her ear. "You will be able to meet my brothers and sisters of the forest!"

Whilst still writing, and sporting the sweetest smile, Sophie answered, "I can't wait!"

Mia addressed the crowd once again.

"Just one mile to the South of where we stand, you will find open ground. There is a pasture where sheep and cows shall roam freely. Nutrition will be provided, and a stream leading to the river will be their constant water source. These animals will not need tending to...they will be free animals who choose to graze upon this land. Here is where the fundamental difference will be...the cows will gladly give their milk whist they are not nursing if you will relieve them of it twice a day. The sheep will require you to keep their coats in order, providing all the wool you will ever need in payment for this service. Do you understand how beautiful this system will be? This is a mutually-agreed-upon way of life, rather than keeping the animals in abject slavery. The animals will be able to come and go as they please, using the pasture when they need assistance. In this way, you will have a steady supply of milk and wool, and the animals will be kept in good health. You have lived without eating the flesh of animals for over of 12 moons, and the taste of meat would now be acrid to you. You must bear this in mind, because the first animals you see will be the easiest to catch and cook."

As Mia was speaking, one such animal appeared from the woods. A cockerel strutted up to and past Mia, then up to the crowd of people, completely unafraid as it pecked and scratched the ground. Not one single person in that crowd saw the cockerel as anything other than a beautifully-plumaged alarm clock, and, something to keep the hens happy. Mia picked up on that communal thought, and her smile lit up her face.

"My friends...I have now passed to all of you the most beautiful gift you will ever own – the gift of Animal Communication. Mother Nature was right in instructing me to do this. You truly are enlightened individuals, and I feel my animals are safe mingling with you good people. Should you need my help, or any further instruction, simply say my name, and I will come to your assistance. We now enter a wonderful time where human and beast are as one."

Mia smiled, then disappeared back to the Realm of Nature, where she would carry on preparing the animals for their return to the Plane of Existence, and a new life with the humans.

Alice looked at Sophie and asked, "Did you get all that?"

"I have written everything down that she said, and I must admit, reading back over my notes, this could be the most exciting time we have had so far! Can you even imagine being able to talk to an animal? To hold a conversation, and know what they are thinking...it is just mind-blowing!" said Sophie.

"I know what you mean! Just think – we will be working with the animals, helping them live a long, active life...not breeding them just for a food source. The addition of milk and eggs to our diets will be a marvellous thing – and all will be gifts from the them, not just taken away because we can. We will be able to ask a hen how she feels, and not just take her eggs...can you imagine that, Sophie?"asked Alice.

"It is unbelievable...and what about the animals we've only known from mythology...can you even imagine speaking with a unicorn? I already thought we were incredibly lucky being saved from the apocalypse – but now this! It's hard to take in, and I'm going to be the one to document it!" said Sophie.

"Yes – we must be very privileged humans. We shall have to live up to Mother's expectations when the animals have fully returned to live alongside us.

Simone Baudelaire walked up to Alice and said, "What do we do while awaiting the animals' return?"

"I believe we have a watermill to build...so, I suggest we all have some breakfast, then join the boys and Wendy in their endeavour," said Alice.

A rather rushed breakfast ensued, and then everybody went to the storeroom to pick up the tools they would work with that day. Making their way to the side of the river, they rendezvoused with Jamie, Michael, Freddie, Jack, and Wendy.

Once again, the people of the commune split into groups...the first group sawed logs, and the second worked with the adzes, to give the round logs two straight edges down their lengths, so that they could sit on top of one another. A third group then fashioned the ends of the logs, so they could be joined to each other. Others carried the finished logs to where the five builders were working, and Jamie, Michael, Freddie, and Jack put each log in place.

Wendy then drove two wooden pins through each log to secure the it to the one underneath. This work had been carrying on for an hour, when the first sighting of an animal occurred. At the edge of the woods, a brown bear sat, watching the builders at work. It displayed no aggression…but was obviously curious as to what was going on. The bear edged a little closer, its curiosity getting the better of its eager mind.

Delphinium stood up upon Sophie's shoulder and whispered in her ear, "Go and say 'hello' to the bear."

Sophie looked at Delphinium, then nodded her head. With a broad smile on her face, she carefully walked over to the large bear, who was still seated, and sat down gently beside him. Everyone held their breaths for a moment, waiting to see what would happen.

"Welcome home!" said Sophie to the bear.

The bear looked at Sophie with a surprised expression on his face. He held out his paw, and Sophie softly took hold of it.

"You speak my tongue!" said the startled animal.

"I am only talking as I normally do, but now, we can all understand each other," explained Sophie.

"May I go catch a fish in your river?" asked the bear politely.

"It is not our river…we can now share everything the world has to offer!"

The bear — still looking slightly bewildered — stood and lumbered into the river, where, within a minute, he had caught his breakfast. As he returned from the river, the bear noticed all the people were now curiously watching him. He showed the crowd his catch, then sat down to eat it. He was in no hurry to make an exit as he felt quite comfortable, because he retained no knowledge of humans ever hunting him, and therefore harboured no aggression towards the group of animals in front of him. He was simply happy to eat his fish, and watch what was going on.

Mina Lester came over to where Alice sat, and placing her kind hand in Alice's she said, "Is this how it will be with all the animals?"

"It appears so, Mina…all of us are beginning anew…including the animals. There can be no more misunderstandings between the human and animal kingdoms, because now there is only one kingdom, and that is the Kingdom of Nature."

Mina liked that answer, and returned to her mother to carry on with their work. Everyone else that that had been watching the event did the same, as the thought of this being a perfectly natural state of events filled their minds. They returned to the tasks they'd been performing before the bear had caught their attention and distracted them.

Jamie Winters was mulling over the plans for the interior of the mill, attempting to work out the height he was going to set the drive shafts . The distance had to be tall enough so the drive shaft was out of anyone's reach on the ground, but a short enough distance from the machine as to not make the drive belt too long. These requirements had two reasons…the first being safety, and the second, because of a lack of materials. A person running a mill could not simply venture out, and kill a cow to replace the leather that was needed for the belt. They had to make the materials they'd been gifted with by Nature last as long as possible…and keeping the drive belts short was the best option for accomplishing this.

Jamie envisioned in his mind's eye the finished mill with its working weaving loom, and a circular saw. The mill would be split in half by a dividing wall. On one side would be Keith's workshop, complete with a circular saw, lathe, and band saw. On the other side of the divide would be Diane's weaving and spinning room. It was quite easy for Jamie to envisage this clearly because the outer and dividing walls had already been erected. Now, it was time to actually fit the drive shafts, and the struts that would hold them in position. Several people began to bring the pieces of equipment

Jamie needed from the storeroom in the safety shelter, and all were laid upon the mill floor in readiness.

The only problem which remained was figuring out how to lift some of the heavier pieces safely into place. Jamie decided to take a break and ponder upon this, leaving the others to ready all the different pieces that needed to be hoisted into position. Jamie strolled into the woods, where he came upon Mia. He bowed his head in respect.

"Lift your gaze, Jamie...I am not Mother Nature," smiled the Unicorn Queen.

"Hello, Mia – we have already made contact with one of your animals," said Jamie.

"I know...I was watching."

"I wish we were as deft with our hands as the bear was...his fishing prowess is amazing! There are many things the bear wishes he could do as well as humans can, too – this would probably be a great way for you and the animals to begin your new lives of trust...by teaching one another. Bearing this in mind, why are you out here contemplating spending many days building a winch device for lifting heavy objects into place? You are missing the obvious answer," said Mia.

"I worry about the safety of such a device, because when I was transported back in time again, I witnessed many disasters with such crude lifting gear."

"The answer is simple...or it will be, when you fully realise what you and the animals can achieve together." As these words left her lips, the answer to Jamie's question joined Mia from the forest behind her.

"May I introduce you to these two elephants, Jamie? Unlike humans, they don't bear names, but I can see that situation changing, as friendships are forged. I think you will find them most helpful," she continued.

"The elephants would be willing to help us?" asked an awe-struck Jamie.

The female elephant lumbered over to where Jamie stood, and placing her trunk around his waist, lifted Jamie onto her back. Jamie's smile was one of a small child seeing an elephant for the first time, and he howled with delight. Mia waved goodbye, as the three new friends trundled through the trees back to the water mill.

"This is wonderful! How can I repay you for your kindness?" asked Jamie.

"You and the humans with you have already thanked us," said the male elephant.

"How? I don't understand..." said Jamie.

"All the human animals that have survived lust not after our tusks, nor do they hunt the other animals of the forest...that is thanks enough. We have waited a long time for the human race to evolve to the point at which you are now, so we may look forward to life on Earth as it should be."

Jamie's smile broadened as they entered the area where the mill was under construction. As he sat high upon his new friend's back, feeling like Tarzan, everyone – including his sister, Alice – looked on in disbelief as Jamie slipped off the massive shoulders of the great beast and jumped to the ground.

"These two magnificent beings are going to help us lift the gear into position...please welcome them as our friends," smiled Jamie.

Everyone stopped what they were doing and lay their work tools down as they gathered round the two elephants. Sophie recorded the event into her journal as Delphinium said to her, "Isn't this wonderful...seeing humans and elephants greeting one another."

"It is one of the most beautiful things I've ever seen," said Sophie, as she scribbled away in her journal.

Without needing encouragement, the two elephants walked over to where the building was under construction and placed their trunks over the wall nearest them, demonstrating what they had in mind. Jamie saw what they were doing, and shouted to Jack Howard and Michael Lester to throw ropes over the elephants' trunks. He then asked Freddie Chambers and Wendy Walters to tie a fixing bracket, onto each of the ropes. Jamie then placed a ladder against the outside wall of where the first bracket was to be attached. He climbed the ladder, carrying in his utility belt, the four nuts and washers to place onto the bolts that were fixed to the brackets. Once he was in position, he asked the first elephant to lift its bracket. As the bracket rose, Freddie Chambers ascended a ladder against the inside wall, and as soon as the bracket was in place, he guided the bolts through the holes. On the other side of the wall Jamie placed a fixing plate over the four bolts, then the washers, followed by the nuts, which he tightened into position. After all four nuts were secure, Jamie asked the elephant to let the rope fall free. He and Freddie repeated the operation with the other elephant, and in no time at all, both drive shaft fixings – complete with bearings – were in place. The elephants then placed their trunks over the wall once more, and Michael and Wendy threw the ropes over their trunks, tying the other ends to the drive shaft, which contained two drive wheels. Jamie – with his ladder – had now moved to the inside of the building, placing his ladder at the opposite wall mount to where Freddie's was. He asked the two elephants to lift once again, and the entire drive shaft rose to where they stood upon their ladders. Once both ends of the drive shaft were through the bearings on the wall mount, two collar fixings were placed at either side of the bearing to prevent the drive shaft from slipping one way or the other; this would restrain the drive shaft from ever moving out of line.

Jamie thanked the two elephants. To his surprise the female elephant asked, "What is this building for?"

"It is a mill for making cloth to produce clothing, furnishings...that sort of thing," said Jamie

"What are those things for?"

Jamie couldn't believe he was in mid-conversation with an elephant, and that she had such a delicate voice.

"We wear the clothes, like this…" said Jamie, as he tugged at the collar of the jumper he was wearing. If you would care to follow us back to the commune, come this way, and I can show you how we use cloth to make furniture and curtains for homes," said Jamie.

"We would like to see that – thank you!" enthused the elephant.

As the morning marched on, it was nearly lunchtime, and everyone was beginning to return to the commune. Mingling amongst them were the two elephants, who were now being questioned by everyone in the excited crowd…each human was desperate to know more about the beautiful creatures at their side.

The elephants revelled in this new friendship, as all thoughts of ivory hunters and been removed from their minds. It didn't take long to reach the commune, and, as promised, Jamie showed them his own log cabin.

Both elephants came to each of the two windows, and pressed an eye up against them to peer inside.

"We have never seen inside a human's den before! Thank you for showing us how you live!" said the male elephant.

"It is our pleasure! You are welcome to visit us anytime, as are all of your friends! We want the whole forest to know we mean no harm to anyone…we look forward to living alongside you and sharing what we have with you, as you have just shared your strength with us. Would you like to stay and eat with us? We are about to make lunch…" asked Jamie.

"Thank you for your kind offer, but we have much to do, and have already eaten," said the elephant.

With that, the two majestic animals trundled back into the forest, and the commune celebrated a morning to remember.

Chapter Ten

osie Anderson was now in charge of the cafeteria. Cooking had been a passion of Josie's for a long time, and working with seasonal vegetables was a great joy, and something she had vast experience in. Josie had always been a vegetarian. Her choice to become one was not political in any way...she was an animal lover, as were all the people that had been saved. As a child, she had been forced to eat meat by overbearing parents, but had never liked its taste or texture – so as an adult, she had learned to produce delicious meals without it. This, of course, made her the perfect choice to be the chef of the commune, as no meat was available to her. Her vast knowledge of protein-enriched, non-meat food was invaluable.

Josie's crew, including herself, numbered ten people in all...each with different levels of knowledge in vegetarian cuisine. In the kitchen, Josie was a born leader, and always had her sleeves rolled up. She and her nine colleagues would venture out each morning, gathering the nuts and fruits for that day's lunch and dinner; the ingredients for breakfast were always picked the night before. A typical day for the canteen staff was a very full one...so much so, it was the only work they did.

Josie Anderson worked closely with Kareem Farmer, as he was discovering new foods daily. Kareem had, in fact, discovered a whole field of rye from which he – with the help of others – had removed the seeds, which were ready to plant as soon as an open field could be found.

Josie looked forward to a time when she would be able to bake bread for the commune, and as the watermill would soon be finished, the building of the necessary windmill wasn't far off. For now, Josie's kitchen was running as smoothly as possible. There had been no complaints about the dishes she was serving, or the way in which they had been cooked, so gastronomically everyone was happy within the commune.

Back at the river, the inside of the watermill was beginning to take shape. Keith Johnson had begun working on the weaving loom, which was to be a permanent fixture within the building. Construction of the roof had been halted, so that everyone could help Keith fit the very large – and heavy – frame of the weaving loom inside. Diane Sanders had asked Keith to build it wide enough to enable her to weave blankets large enough to go on a double bed. She knew that in the long run, this would save time.

Diane Sanders' four sewing machines had also been fixed to a bench, and their drive wheels made ready to accept power from the water wheel when the building was complete. The spinning wheel that Keith had made earlier had also been brought into Diane's area of the workshop. This had also been modified to receive power from the watermill. On the other side of the wall, Keith's lathe had been adapted so it could work within the higher tolerance of water power. Along the back wall, Keith had fashioned a workbench, which held a circular saw that he would be able to make planks of wood with. In turn these planks of wood would be used on the windmill, as soon as the watermill was finished. The last piece of equipment was a band saw, which Keith had managed to connect to the new power source.

Within a day, the heavier work upon the loom was completed, then the fitting of the intricate working parts and the placing of all the strings could begin. Keith found this phase of the work relaxing, and after attaching all the working parts he had prepared earlier, the loom was up and running in no time at all. In fact, the completion of the loom brought Dianes' half of the mill's work to a close. Lastly, Freddie, Jack, Michael, and Wendy would be fitting the power supply with all the linkages which passed the power of the water through the gearing system, then onto the separate machines. Whilst they they got on with that task, Jamie Winters, his sister Alice, and Keith Johnson visited the site which had been prepared for the windmill.

"There will be no need for me to build this structure out of logs, as my circular saw will be up and running as soon as the roof goes over the watermill. The wheel itself is being fashioned to your specifications, Jamie, and has already been attached to the shaft. I can start to build this structure as soon as the watermill is complete, as I will have the ability to make planks of wood, and so, keep to the original design. When do you think the water wheel will be attached, and the mill up and running?" asked Keith.

"The wheel will be affixed as soon as the roof goes on, and as you know, they are doing that as we speak...I would say that the mill will be working within a few days," said Jamie.

"Everything is moving so fast! This is a very exciting time," exclaimed Alice.

"Yes...it is, sis...you've just given me an idea," said Jamie.

"What's that?" asked Keith.

"One thing I can do is govern the water flow underneath the wheel. In ancient times, problems occurred when the river ran too fast or too slow...much of the time, their machines could not compensate with the correct speeds for most of the time. I will make it so that we can adjust the flow of the river in such a way that our wheel turns at a uniform rate of our choosing all of the time," said Jamie.

"Do you have a design for that, Jamie?" asked Alice.

"I can see it in my mind's eye...I just need to get it on paper so I can check my theory," answered Jamie. He suddenly felt a bulge within the back pocket of his trousers.

Alice smiled, as she had just received a message from Mother Nature. "Jamie...if you would care to check your back pocket?" suggested Alice.

Jamie reached into his back pocket, and pulled out a folded piece of paper. As he unfolded it several times, he saw that upon the white sheet of paper were the plans he had in his head...however, this plan included the dimensions of the locks and sluices required to make it work, which would give him a controlled stream of water at all times. The only time the mill would not be in use was when the river was still...and that was very seldom, indeed.

Jamie looked up from surveying the plans with a wide grin and said, "Thank Mother Nature for me – this is brilliant!"

Alice just nodded her head, smiled, and said, "It is done."

All three returned to the watermill, and Jamie excitedly showed the new development to his four companions. "I will head a team of workers to begin excavating. As soon as you are ready to fit the wheel and gearing let me know, and I will go ask Mia for help again." With that, Jamie left the main building, and requested 12 volunteers to go with him a short way upstream to begin marking out the trench which would lead the water to the power wheel. The wheel could not be placed directly into the currents of the River Aire without sustaining massive damage during rapidly-flowing periods...and it would hardly move whilst the river was flowing slowly.

Two of the 12 volunteers taking part in the excavation of the trench were Steve Bingham and Tom Harper. Steve heard a noise emitting from a wooded area. He said to Tom, "Did you hear that?"

Tom nodded his head, then said, "Let's investigate, and see what it is."

Both men put down their shovels and followed the sound into the woods, which increased in volume as they edged closer.

They both peered over the edge of a large rock lying on the ground, and were shocked to see a horse with its back leg trapped between two exposed tree roots.

"What kind of horse is that?" gawped Steve.

"You know what kind of horse that is," snorted Tom.

"Yes, I do...but I wanted to make sure you are seeing the same thing as I am..."

"It's a unicorn!" exclaimed Tom.

"Well...I'm glad we've have sorted that out! Now...can you help me please?" said the pure-white stallion unicorn.

Tom and Steve both gasped as they heard the magnificent being speak. Both men, dumbfounded, nodded their heads, and moved to where the unicorn was standing. Tom stroked the unicorn's silken mane, and said, "Hello."

"Hello to you my, friend...I do so appreciate you helping me out this way."

"Think nothing of it! If you would excuse me, I will just help my partner to free your leg," said Tom.

Tom joined Steve at the unicorn's forelock, and Steve said, "If you pull on that root, I will pull on this one, then his leg will be freed."

Both men tugged with all their might, and the two roots gave just enough for the unicorn to pull his leg free.

The unicorn reared up onto his hind legs in delight of being free. The magnificent animal then looked at the two humans that had helped him and said, "You are very kind, and I thank you for your help. If I can be of service to you, please let me know."

"I shall take care of that, Gustaf," said Mia, as she appeared where they all stood.

"Milady," nodded Gustaf, as he turned and walked away.

"That was a unicorn – wasn't it?" said a thrilled Steve Bingham.

"Indeed, it was...and the two of you could have been scared, and just left him there...but without thought for your own safety, you helped him. You have, in fact, just helped the leader of the unicorns – one so powerful he could have run both of you through with his horn at the same time...but instead of running, you stayed and helped him. If you would follow me, someone would like to meet you.

Mia and her two companions delved deeper into the woods. Sitting on an altar amid a circle of upright stones, Mother Nature and Alice Winters-Chambers awaited their arrival. To Alice's left stood Sophie Narey with her journal in hand, and Delphinium upon her shoulder. The two men were brought before Mother Nature, and the Goddess held out her hands so that they might take them.

"Thank you, Mia, for bringing these two wonderful boys to me...and thank you, Tom Harper, and Steve Bingham, for what you did for one of my animals."

Steve was about to say something, but Alice put her finger to her lips to shush him.

"I have summoned you here firstly, to thank you, and secondly, to ask for your help in the rebuilding of humanity.

"I have no knowledge of pleasuring a woman to that end..." blurted Steve awkwardly.

"Nor do I – but we will both try our best to do as you ask," nodded Tom.

Steve gulped as he thought of trying to have sex with a woman, and looked very worried.

"Be still, my children...in your New World, no one shall be asked to perform things they are unequipped either mentally or physically to deliver. Viktoria and Linda Harper are both pregnant, but neither of them had to forgo their rights to their lifestyle to become so."

"I am to be an uncle?" said a delighted Tom, his eyes beginning to water.

"You now have the opportunity to become more than that...should you wish it," said Mother Nature.

"How so?" asked a befuddled Steve.

Sophie Narey was scribbling as fast as she could in her journal.

"Join me upon this altar, and I will extract from you your life-giving sperm – which I will unite with an egg from Viktoria for Tom, and an egg from Linda for Steve. The new lives will gestate within me, and when the time comes, I will birth and gift the children to you both...this way you will be the children's blood fathers without compromising your way of life."

Both men were speechless, but managed to nod their heads in unison.

"In that case, remove your clothing."

Both men disrobed within seconds of being asked to do so, and sat at either side of Mother Nature. She placed her hands on both men's penises; the effect was instantaneous, and both men's sexual organs grew very hard. Mother Nature squeezed gently, and sperm gushed into her hands. She then lapped the juice from both hands as the two men passed out on the altar. Mia and the Goddess disappeared, and Alice and Sophie ran to the two men, who were just waking up.

"Are you ok?" asked Alice.

"I'm fine...I feel the need to apologize for what I have standing to attention in my groin, though..." said a blushing Tom.

"No need at all! You are both beautiful, and a sight to behold right now! Tell me...how do you feel about what has just taken place?" asked Alice. Sophie continued scribbling away.

"It's strange to try and put into words what we are thinking right now...will it be possible for all men like us to have children this way?" marvelled Steve.

"Yes, it will – now, there will be no difference between being gay, lesbian, or straight, as everyone can reproduce thanks to Mother Nature," informed Alice.

"In that case, we really have evolved from an undeveloped world into an enlightened one," said Tom.

"Indeed, we have..." agreed Alice, a smile of contentment adorning her face. "Indeed, we have."

Back at the side of the river, the work had carried on to such a degree that the definitive shape of what they were trying to achieve had become clear to see. Beginning only three feet short of the river was a series of rectangular holes – four in number – the first one measuring 12 x 6 x 4 feet, becoming progressively smaller, each one joined with appropriately-sized pipes which were provided with the gearing. The entire commune had joined in with the work since Tom and Steve had left...and the result was staggering.

A group of people had already begun lining the holes with logs. The bedrock was dense enough to hold water, so linings were not needed at the bottom. In each consecutive hole which had been dug, the bedrock level deepened accordingly. The millpond itself was already in situ, in the guise of a very large, shallow depression in the ground that held water to the side of the Watermill.

Tom and Steve returned to the commune, reporting back to Michael. He asked them to join himself, Freddie, Jack, Jamie, and Wendy to help bring the waterwheel from where Keith had made it to the side of the watermill. The paddles of the wheel were fashioned from logs, split in half and each about 2½ feet long. These were attached on both sides to very large wheels, and the middle of the wheel was fixed to a spindle. The spindle itself was joined to an eight-foot-long log which had been shaped and would act as the drive shaft.

Keith Johnson knew that the drive shaft would need to be replaced quite often...as yet, he had no means of making bearings, so the shaft was keyed at both ends for easy detachment from the water and drive wheels. Keith already possessed two such replacement shafts, which were stored in the watermill itself. The waterwheel was located 50 yards from the millpond, and Keith had built it upon a trestle which was fitted with six handmade wheels and axles – the entirety of which was now ready to be pulled to the pond. At this stage, any member of the team could have called upon the elephants to come and drag the mighty wheel to the pond...but as this was something that the humans could do on their own, they did it themselves. Alice did not want Mother Nature thinking they would simply use the animals whenever they saw fit, as that would be repeating history, and placing the animals in a servant role...and that just wouldn't do.

Two ropes had been fixed to the front of the trestle holding the waterwheel, and these would be used to move the structure. The entire company of the commune took hold of a rope, or attached themselves to the trestle, so they could push the device ancient Egyptian-style. The waterwheel began to move towards its destination, as the people pulled and pushed in unison. Two ropes trailed from the back of the trestle so the people pulling would be able to go behind the wheel, preventing it from running out of control as it descended the slope into the dry hole when they reached the millpond.

The whole operation went as smoothly as everything else that the enlightened humans had undertaken. Behind the scenes, an army of muses and fairy folk had been invisibly working throughout – from the first log cabin to this initial mill of Nature Industries. The end result would be a belief that as a team, they could achieve anything...the human animal had finally learned that there was no 'I' in team.

The waterwheel now lay at the side of the mill, ready to be lifted into place, when the trumpeting sounds of elephants resonated in everyone's ears – only this time, it wasn't just the elephants.

Mia strode to the edge of the millpond, and from behind her poured a multitude of beasts. Every animal edged around the pond, and stood upon its banks. This spectacle took the breath of the entire commune, all of whom were in the dry pond. As they gazed around the banks of the pond, they saw lions, tigers, elephants, deer – even a giraffe – but the beings that held the attention of the group were the centaurs, unicorns, minotaurs, and all the animals believed to be extinct.

Mia regally walked into the pond and up to the gathering, saying, "Now is the time for everyone to meet. I have brought with me all the leaders of the animal kingdom, so that you all may sit down and discuss the future together, after which, you can finish Mother's first mill.

The delegation of animals joined the humans in the dry pond, and the first-ever meeting of its kind took place on that historic day. Without a doubt, the busiest person there was Sophie Narey, as she was writing down everything that was being said. Delphinium was industrious as well, keeping her quill full of ink.

The meeting was quite eventful, as guidelines for behaviour were set, and rules to guide both animals and humans were drawn up. There was no underhanded wording; everything was out in the open, and a path was laid and set in motion for harmony to exist between the animal and human kingdoms. It wouldn't be long before there was no human or animal kingdom – there would only be the Kingdom of Nature – where no one ruled, and no one was persecuted. Utopia would finally be found...and everyone – human and animal alike – would speak the same language, and live their lives without fear.

Jamie decided that this occurrence was far too monumental for everyone to return to work, so he shouted out at the top of his voice,

"Let's celebrate this wonderful day by throwing a party in honour of our new friends!"

Everybody was definitely up for that, so they all – humans and animals alike – made their way back to the commune, and had a great time. From her vantage point within the Realm of Nature, the Goddess recalled all of her muses and Mia, for their work was complete. From now on, the muses could perform their work from within the confines of their own realm, leaving the new human race – with its enlightened outlook – to carry on their lives in their New World.

Mother Nature called Alice to her domain.

"Alice, my child...come – sit with me."

"Thank you, Mother. Why am I here?"

"This is now your time, Alice...you have achieved everything I asked of you, and it is time for you to lead on your own. I have recalled my muses, to let life continue as it should."

"Does this mean I won't see you again?" worried Alice.

"I will always be within your psyche, and am always on hand to help with your decisions. Everything I granted you still exists...you and Sophie – along with Delphinium – will still be able to travel the world to keep things in order," said the Goddess.

"But I thought you said you had retracted all your muses, and the like..." said Alice.

"Indeed, I have – but Delphinium is different. There are two reasons for which she shall remain in your world...her duty keeping Sophie's quill filled with ink, and the promise she made Sophie that she would stay with her for as long as she wanted her to stay."

"I see...I don't suppose you would stay if I asked you to?" hoped Alice.

"Alice, my child, I will always be with you...trust me on that. I will always guide your decisions – on that you have my word."

Alice suddenly found herself back in the commune, perfectly happy celebrating with her new animal friends. The only thoughts that remained in her head were ones of the future, and the protection of the planet.

Alice joined in the fun, and she and Freddie danced the night away knowing that tomorrow was a big day...one which would see her first mill beginning producing cloth and planks of wood.

Chapter Eleven

The daybreak was as spectacular as any witnessed thus far, and the accompanying birdsong made the mood of the commune full of expectations for the day ahead. Everyone made their way to the dry millpond after they had eaten breakfast. When they arrived at the site, they found they were not the only ones eager to make a start...a good few of the animals they'd met the previous day were waiting for them to arrive.

A centaur approached Alice and said, "We offer our assistance with your endeavours."
"Thank you very much!" smiled Alice shaking his hand. "You are most welcome here!" she continued.

The same two elephants manoeuvred themselves into position by the waterwheel as Freddie and Jack tied ropes to the top of the wheel, then making loops at the other ends to place around the elephants' trunks. Both magnificent beasts raised their heads and trunks, and the large wheel rose effortlessly into the air after Keith had released it from the fixings on the trestle.

Keith and Jamie placed a ladder at either side of the orifice the driveshaft was going through, climbing to the opening in the wall, Michael instructed the elephants to begin walking towards the awaiting mount. From their positions on the ladders, Keith and

Jamie guided the driveshaft through the hole. Both men climbed down their ladders, took them inside the mill, and placed them on either side of the hole, as before. They grasped the rope which was attached to the drive wheel, and throwing it over their shoulders as they climbed the ladders. Once they reached the tops of their ladders they were past where the driveshaft would enter the wall. Above the hole were two pullies, which both men place their ropes through, letting the ropes drop to the ground, were Wendy and Simone awaited. Jamie and Keith descended their ladders until they reached the hole, then shouted that they were ready.

The elephants began to slowly inch forward as the driveshaft entered the hole. The two women began to raise the drive wheel, and Keith fitted a collar to the driveshaft to prevent the waterwheel withdrawing the shaft back out of the wall. The large drive wheel that Wendy and Simone were lifting was now at the correct height. Jamie and Keith slotted it into position, then Keith hammered the holding keys into place, and the work was complete.

Keith, Jamie, Wendy, and Simone all ran back outside to see the finished waterwheel in place...and what a spectacular sight it was! Yet another joint venture between the animals and humans had been undertaken, with spectacular results. As with all things, what had taken place in what used to be Leeds – such as the construction of the watermill, and the meeting with the animals – had also occurred all over the world, with the same degree of success.

The centaur who was standing with Alice offered his congratulations on a job well done. "As you can see, Alice...a wondrous future stretches out before us...as long as we can live and work in harmony together."
"Sharing our lives with other animals is one of Humanity's greatest prizes, and will always be looked upon as such. I see

great things in the future, as we all continue to learn from one another," said Alice, as Michael walked past her and shouted to her brother.

"Jamie – now, it's up to you to fit the gearing whilst we finish the feed ponds!"

"Indeed, it is! Freddie – come with me, please, to help gear the drive," said Jamie.

"Righty-ho!" smiled Freddy.

"Everyone else...follow us to the ponds!" called Wendy.

"How am I going to log this? I can't be in two places at once!" said Sophie.

Delphinium stood on her shoulder and said, "I will go with the others, and relay to you what they are doing."

"Thank you Delphinium!" smiled Sophie.

Delphinium kissed Sophie on the cheek, then flew off with the others.

Just to the North of where the watermill was being constructed, the large shadow of a flying creature moved across the land. This was a shadow from the past...a shadow from mythology...for casting this silhouette was a magnificent dragon. Mythology had proven to be quite accurate, in some respects, because this beastie looked exactly like the pictures in books that used to exist before the Apocalypse. Unlike the depictions, however, dragons did not breathe fire – nor did they covet maidens. They were, in fact, highly intelligent beings...beings far more advanced than humans.

The particular dragon that was flying towards the settlement was the new leader of his kind, as the previous one had discovered – to his cost – not to cross Mother Nature. In fairness, all dragons which had been placed in the part of the world where Alice and her commune existed were happy about the situation, because the previous leader had always been outspoken, and liked to speak of war. There was no cause for such thoughts in this modern era, so the new leader was planning to first meet the humans, then explain that they all only desired to co-exist. The dragons wished to live their lives in peace upon the New Earth...something which had never been achieved in the past.

Whilst lining the last filler pond with wooden logs, someone shouted out, "Look up at the sky!"

Everyone stopped what they were doing as the dragon swooped down and landed in the middle of the dry millpond.

"I bring you greetings from all of my kind," said the dragon, in a deeply eloquent voice. His words seemed to echo in the silence, as he retracted its wings.

Everyone shuffled uneasily, as the massive, multi-coloured dragon waited for a response. Alice swiftly rescued the moment, and strode towards the dragon, unafraid. "On behalf of everyone here, I bid you welcome!"

"Do you have a spring, so that I might drink? I can only drink volcanic, or natural spring water..." asked the dragon.

"We have not found a spring, as yet, I'm afraid..." answered Alice.

"Do you mind if I seek one out for you, so that I may drink from it?"

"You are most welcome to do that," smiled Alice.

The dragon leapt up into the air, and opened its wings to fly. It soared into the sky, then dove down to a location just behind the commune...In fact, he landed not 50 meters from the canteen. Alice and a few others ran to where the dragon had descended, and there – surrounded by rocks jutting up from the ground – stood the dragon, lapping from a rock pool that had running water entering it from one of the rocks above.

"Beautiful, crystal-clear water! It tastes as if it was purified through volcanic rock...but I see no volcano," said the dragon.

"I seem to recall that in the distant past a volcano once stood in this area," said Alice.

"If I were you, I would always drink from this spring, and leave the river water to the fish," said the dragon.

"How can we thank you for finding this spring?" asked Alice.

"You could allow my people to drink from it," suggested the dragon.

"This water does not belong to us...anyone can drink from it!" said Alice.

"And...you won't chase us away?" marvelled the dragon.

"Of course not! Why would we do that? Your people are welcome anytime...we will gladly share whatever we have."

"You are very kind...do you have a name?"

"I am known as Alice."

The dragon lowered his head and said, "Forgive me – I knew not that I was speaking with The Alice..."

"Not 'The Alice'...just Alice. Now – please, raise your head."

"You are the one who convinced Mother to give us all a second chance...my people would do anything you ask of them, milady."

Jamie leaned over and whispered into Alice's ear, "So...dragons bow down in front of my weird sister!"

Alice gave Jamie a nudge with her elbow as he chuckled.

"All I ask for is for your friendship...will you bring your people to meet us?" said an excited Alice.

"It would be my – and my people's – greatest pleasure to do so," said the dragon, as he took off in the direction of his awaiting clan.

Everyone went back to the pond, and returned to work. Jamie went inside and joined Freddie, who was configuring the gearing between the drive shaft – which was connected to the waterwheel itself – and the flywheel which was attached to the drive shaft that was fitted to the wall.

"Freddie – you will never believe what I've just seen."

"Nothing could impress me in this day and age...we see spectacular new things daily, it seems..." said an unimpressed Freddie.

"I have just witnessed my sister – your lovely wife – talking to a dragon!"

"What?!" gawped Freddie.

"You heard me...a dragon!"

"I retract my previous statement – I am very impressed! Did anyone get burned?"

"There was no breathing of fire...I think that might be a fairy tale...but then again, I thought dragons were fairy tales..."

"I think the term 'fairy tale' was abolished when Sophie Neary's new friend appeared – then after her, several muses...the odd unicorn or two...not to mention people that are half horse, half human – whatever they are called," quipped Freddie.

"They are called centaurs, Freddie..."

"Yes, well, I do believe you take my point."

"Indeed, I do. Now how are we doing with these gears?"

"I do like that term, 'we'; I have done quite well so far...but now that you are finally here, can you tell me why cog four doesn't marry to cog five?"

"I did notice that three of the cogs were labelled wrong...I meant to put that right," remarked Jamie.

"Please...tell me they are not the ones I have already fitted!" begged Freddie, with his eyes closed tight.

"They are not the ones you have already fitted," laughed Jamie, much to his friend's relief.

"With adjustments, the way you have done this, it will work, but not very efficiently. This is why I altered the numbering of the separate gears. When I was sent back to mediaeval times to learn about natural power, I could see the primitive gearing was wrong...but obviously, I could not tell them how to make it right."

"The space-time continuum," said Freddie.

"Indeed – had I done that the Industrial Revolution would have unfolded differently – and I couldn't chance that. But here and now in the New World, I can put that right. If you would just help me lift this gear and place it where you were trying to fit the other onto the bar, you will find it marries quite well, as the first three you've attached are different to how they should have been," said Jamie.

"Now...all becomes clear," said Freddie mystically, as he helped his friend lift the large gear and place it onto the bar.

The gear fit perfectly, as did the rest when they were slotted into place. The last cog was attached to a drive wheel. From that wheel a belt would be joined to the main drive wheel, which was fitted to the drive shaft. The watermill was now ready to deliver power to all of the machines within the mill...all that was needed bring it to life was flowing water.

Outside, the millpond, sluices, and water gates were ready to accept the water from the river...all that was required was the removal of 3 feet of earth between the riverbank and the first of the ponds.

Two centaurs approached the riverbank then stood in the river, and both began kicking vigorously at the bank towards the first watertight gate. As their strong hooves gouged into the side of the river, water began filling the space they had dug. Both centaurs laughed out loudly as the splashing water drenched everyone nearby. When they reached the point where they were nine or ten inches away from the gate, the power of the running water removed the last of the soil, and the watertight gate held, even though there was no water behind it offering support. The crowd of people cheered as the two extremely-muddy centaurs exited the water and began to shake themselves dry – which further drenched the onlookers.

Simone Baudelaire ran back to the watermill to inform Jamie and Freddie that they were ready to open the first gate.

"Are you ready for the gate to be opened, Jamie?!" she shouted.
"We have just fitted the main drive belt, so yes...the mill is ready to receive water. We will come back with you to watch the proceedings," said Jamie.

Sophie Neary closed her journal to return and meet up with Delphinium...and witness the event herself.

All the gates following the first one were in an open position. They worked like canal lock gates, as there would always be water on both sides of them, so they would be easy to open and close. The gate by the river was the strongest of them all, and it functioned like a sluice gate. Jack Howard and Michael Lester had built this gate, having worked out beforehand that no amount of strength they could muster would allow the gate to open outwards into the river. That was the reason they'd come up with the sluice gate idea. All the while they were constructing the gate, there was a nagging doubt about the possibility of it being unable to open, because the force of the water from the outside of the gate would place enormous pressure upon it, driving it violently against the inner slide mount. The arrival of the animals – in particular the elephants – alleviated that problem. Large ring-holders had been bolted into position at the bottom outside edge of the door. Attached to these thick rings were ropes, which passed over two large pullies attached to the outside posts. The ropes went through the pullies, and were secured to both elephants to enable them to pull the door open for the first time. After that first opening, the door would become easier to open and close using the winding mechanism with crank handles which had been attached to both sides, as it would have water on either side every time thereafter.

Wendy Walters had climbed onto the elephant at the right-hand side of the door, whilst Simone Baudelaire had mounted the one on the left. Both women looked at Alice as they awaited her go-ahead. Alice looked at her brother, her husband, Michael Lester, and Jack Howard...all of whom gave the thumbs-up to go ahead. Alice shouted to Wendy and Simone to begin. Both women whispered into the ears of their elephants asking them to move forward. The two ropes tightened and creaked...they were clearly straining as the elephants inched forward, away from each other. There was a tense moment when nothing was moving; all that could be heard was the creaking and groaning of the ropes.

Suddenly, someone shouted, "The crank handles are moving!" No sooner had the words left their lips when water began to gush from the bottom of the door, and thousands of gallons of river water rushed through the bottom opening of the gate. As this happened, the door began to move more freely, and the elephants walked away. The crank handles began to spin as the door lifted and opened fully.

Water blazed a trail into the first pond and it rapidly filled, then down to the second and third, as they filled at the same speed as the first, continuing on towards the waterwheel. The wheel itself was set in a freely-rotating mode, as Jamie had known the water's initial power would smash everything they had done. As expected, when the water connected with the wheel, it began to spin uncontrollably.

Jamie looked at Freddie and said, "We need to cool the spindle down, or else it will burn!"

Jamie and Freddie had foreseen this problem, and had fashioned a makeshift tube using the stripped bark of discarded logs which led to the spindle. This was located adjacent to the second pond and awaited its end to be placed into the flowing water. The water rushed through the tube at great speed and was deposited straight onto the spindle, producing vast plumes of steam as it did its job perfectly.

"Now...that was a clever idea!" smiled Jack Howard.

Jamie and Freddie smiled back at him and they shook hands, feeling quite pleased with themselves.

The water was now gushing past the wheel into the millpond; it took three hours for the pond to fill. The crude cooling system worked well as the steam dissipated and the spindle slowed. At the far left-hand side of the millpond was a cut back to the river, which would keep a constant flow of water at all times so the pond would not become stagnant. As water began to fill this channel that led back to the river, the wheel turned at a normal pace.

With the river flowing normally, all gates were in a fully-open position. If the river should slow down, the gates would be half-closed, causing pressure to build up so that the wheel would not slow down. If the river flowed too quickly, or in the case of a flood, all gates would be closed, and work would cease for safety reasons. In the New World, safety would always come first.

As if in approval by Nature, a group of otters made their way up the cut from the river, claiming the millpond as their new home.

Jamie, Freddie, Jack, Simone, Jasmine, Michael, Wendy, Mina, Keith, Diane, and Sophie – with Delphinium on her shoulder – all took position in the watermill as Alice stood by the mechanism that shifted the drive belt from the freewheel to the drive wheel. She placed her fingers around the handle and said, "Are you ready for me to engage the belt?"

Jamie gave her the go-ahead, and Alice pulled the lever. The drive belt slipped a little at first, but then grabbed the wheel as the whole mechanism began to turn. Everyone looked up at the driveshaft as it began to spin. The mill wasn't very wide, so there was little torque between the two drive wheels, with the one nearest the drive belt turning a few seconds before the one furthest away began spin. Soon, both drive wheels were revolving at the same constant speed. The first one had a belt which connected to Diane's weaving loom...at the moment, this belt was attached to a free wheel which spun, adjacent to a fixed wheel that was stationary. On the other side of the free wheel was a second stationary wheel...this wheel was connected to a drive wheel located at the end of a line of sewing machines. As soon as Diane moved the drive belt onto her fixed wheel, the loom burst into life as did the drive wheel by the sewing machines.

Everyone clapped with delight as all their hard work paid off. Keith then opened a door and entered his woodwork room. Above the circular saw was another drive shaft, which was connected by a belt to the second drive wheel in Diane's room. Fitted to this shaft were two drive wheels – one connected to the circular saw, the other to a bandsaw. Both had the same arrangement with the free and fixed wheels, and worked exactly like Diane's.

The watermill was a complete success, and everyone involved took great pride in a job well done...an endeavour which cost nothing to build, made by workers who expected no payment. The new system was working – and it was working well.

Jamie was thrilled that his knowledge garnered in the 16th century had made all this possible. Suddenly he turned to Freddie and said, "I feel strange...I'm going outside for some fresh air."

As he ventured out, he saw the same Goddess that had sent him on his journeys of discovery. He walked up to her and said with a smile on his face, "Does this meet with your approval?"

"Again, Jamie Winters, you have done well, and your hard work despite all you have been put through has come to fruition. In answer to your question – the mill is perfect – as, I am sure, the windmill will be. With this in mind, I will now deliver on a promise that I made your wonderful sister."

Mother Nature lifted her staff, pointing it to her left-hand side; as a bubble of mist appeared. She then repeated the action on her right-hand side the same thing occurred. As the mist to her right cleared, Jamie's eyes filled with tears of joy, as his beautiful bride-to-be Laura Dinsdale was now standing where the mist had been. Jamie picked her up in his arms, and twirled her around. As he looked to Mother Nature's left, standing there were Laura's two children. His family had returned, after spending over 300 years in limbo within the Realm of Nature.

Mother Nature beamed as she said to Jamie Winters, "Enjoy your life together."

Jamie thanked the Goddess as she disappeared, then took his little family to meet everyone. Every person in the commune somehow knew Laura...and she knew them. Life carried on as if she had been there from the beginning, as the Goddess had gifted that memory into the minds of everyone connected.

JOHN PAUL BERNETT

Chapter Twelve

osie Anderson – along with three others from the canteen – was collecting water from the spring alongside three dragons who were taking a drink. Josie suddenly stopped filling her vessel, and turned to listen to the sweetest singing she had ever heard. When she looked behind her, she saw it was a female dragon singing, sitting beside another dragon who was helping her baby partake from the water hole. Josie walked over to the her and smiled. "What a beautiful singing voice you have! What is your song about?"

The female dragon had tears in her eyes when solemnly she answered, "It is a song of loss...the loss of my child."

"Oh...I'm so sorry. May I ask – how did you lose your child?"

"Like most of us lose our children...they fall from our clutches to their death as we try to take them to the water," explained the dragon.

"That is awful, can you not nest closer to the water?" suggested Josie.

"No...the water always belongs to someone else...and nobody wants dragons near them," said the despondent dragon.

"That is nonsense! Please...would you ask your leader to visit Alice straight away?"

"I am here...but what she says is true. People have always feared us...yet we know not why," came the deep voice of the dragon's leader as he lifted his head from the pool of water.

"Would you come with me, please, so that we may talk with Alice?"

"It would be an honour to do so," said the dragon.

When Josie and her new friend found Alice, she was speaking with Kareem Farmer about his plan to grow a crop of rye with which Josie could make bread.

"Can I have a word with you, Alice?" said Josie.

"Of course you can!" said Alice, with her usual convivial smile.

"I was chatting with a female dragon at the water hole, and she informed me that they lose a lot of young babies whilst they are flying as they try to bring them to drink."

"Why don't they nest closer to the water hole?" asked Alice.

"That is what I said...but the poor things are under the impression that we wouldn't want them to be close to us," said Josie.

"Is this true?" asked a shocked Alice of the dragon leader.

"We have always been chased away, malady," said the dragon in shame as he lowered his head.

"We must do something about this! We cannot afford to lose any babies if we are going to replenish the Earth," said Alice.

"You speak of us as if we are your equal..." said the astounded dragon.

"You are our equal...everyone is now equal, and that is the way it shall stay. Now...why do you lose your babies?"

"Our arms are too short to hold them, and their claws are too small to grasp our scales. They simply fall from our arms to the ground below," said the forlorn dragon.

"I understand...this means no more flying for the babies. How many eggs and babies do you have at the moment?" enquired Alice.

"We have two eggs, and three babies."

"In that case, I need 5 dragons that are strong enough to carry humans – two holding eggs, and three holding babies. Can you do this for me, as quickly as possible? We certainly cannot lose anymore dragons," said Alice.

"I will return with four other's within the hour milady."

"I shall find four others to assist me. Josie – will you help carry a dragon baby?"

"It would be an honour, Alice."

"Off you go then – and be back soon!" called Alice, as the three dragons flew away.

Alice and Josie walked back to the commune, Alice said to Josie, "I'm glad you brought that to my attention! Now, if you would kindly inform your people they will have to do without you for a while, I shall find three more volunteers."

"Volunteers for what?" interjected Jamie, who was within earshot of the conversation.

"Volunteers to fly with a dragon to its lair then carry back their young, so they may all move closer to the spring," informed Alice.

"Nevermind all the rest of what you just said...you had Freddy and me the second you said 'fly with a dragon'," said Jamie.

"I just need one more, in that case..." said Alice.

"Did I hear you right? Did you just say, 'fly with a dragon'?" gaped Jack Howard.

"I did, indeed..." smiled Alice.

"Well – that's my bucket list completed...being able to produce light from my fingertips...flying a dragon...Yep! My list is complete!" quipped Jack, grinning like the Cheshire cat.

"In that case, we are ready. As soon as the dragons return we will go," nodded Alice.

It didn't take long for the dragons to return, and as all five landed, their intrepid would-be flyers walked up to them. Alice had visited Diane in the watermill, and she had quickly fashioned five slings which were large enough to hold baby dragons – and eggs.

The dragons knelt down in front of the five lucky people, who then climbed onto the necks of the enchanted beasts. Each dragon asked their rider if they were comfortable, and to hold on tightly. As if in a fixed formation, all five dragons leapt into the air and outstretched their wings. The feeling was beyond anything any of the passengers had ever experienced before.

In a line, following the leader of the dragons, they all encircled the commune...and for the first time, Alice bore witness to all the work they had accomplished from the sky. Her heart nearly burst with pride when she saw how grand it looked...but pride was for another day. Now, it was time for fun, and she and her friends were flying dragons – there wasn't anything she could think of that would ever top the feeling she had at that moment in time.

After circling the commune, they veered off in a line, following their leader towards where the dragons nested. It was a good way off from the commune, and took fifteen minutes to reach flying quickly in a straight line. Alice and her friends were surprised to see how much woodland now covered their part of the world.

The five dragons began to descend into their nesting area, as one landed after another. All five riders dismounted as the entire clan encircled them.

"Hello, everyone!" greeted Alice with her ingratiating smile.

"What you are prepared to do for us, and our young, is wonderful..." said one of the female dragons.

"It is our pleasure," said Alice, bowing her head slightly.

The clan of dragons could not believe a human would bow in their presence, and show them such a level of respect. The dragons mirrored her actions, watching on in trepidation...and hope.

"You shall soon grow tired of doing this every day, I fear..." uttered their leader.

"No – you misunderstand my intentions – I mean to move you all from this place, and hope you will take residence by the water fountain near our commune," answered Alice.

The dragons looked at one another in shock as their startled leader said, "You would have all of us live so close to your people?"

"Of course – that is the idea – these young ones need to be near water, and not have to risk their lives in the pursuit of such," answered Alice.

The company of dragons all had an excited look about their demeanour, as their leader told them, "Go...gather what you need...we are moving this very day." He then turned to Alice and said, "No human has ever done such a wondrous thing for my kind...how can we repay you?"

"By accepting my offer, and telling all of your friends – whatever species of animal they may be – that all are welcome to coexist with us, and share in what we have," said Alice.

In the trees above the humans and dragons, a group of fairies were listening to the conversation that had just taken place, and had been filled with hope. They all agreed that the centaurs and unicorns should hear of the great deed done by the Queen of the Humans. They all flew off in the direction of the unicorns.

Within the Realm of Nature, the Goddess and Mia had been watching the events unfold. Mother Nature said, "It was a great day when I found that girl...she is proving to be a more honest and just leader than I ever envisaged."

"She is honest, and just; add to that loving, and approachable, and you have our Alice. My unicorns love her and her kind – and after today, even the skeptical minotaurs will mellow to her...she is perfect in every way," answered Mia.

Back upon the Plane of Existence, Alice and Josie cradled the two large, multi-coloured eggs within their special pouches as they climbed back onto the dragons that had brought them, whilst Jack, Jamie, and Freddie picked up a baby dragon each. As four riders safe with their treasures sat at the ready, Freddie struggled with the feisty little young male. Every time he placed the playful baby in his waiting pouch, he exited quickly in the moment it took Freddie to turn to mount his ride. Alice laughed and dismounted, speaking softly to the excited little creature, as he raised his prcious tiny arms to be lifted into hers. After a kiss and a cuddle, he went as good as gold into his pouch, curling into a small green ball. "Takes a woman's touch..." she said with a laugh. The dragon leader let out a rare snort of amusement, and with Alice upon his back, asked if everyone was ready. They all gave the ok, as they leapt into the air and began to flap their wings. The sound of 30 dragons taking to flight was deafening, but it must have made a magnificent sight, as they flew off in a V-formation behind their leader with their new champion Alice Winters-Chambers.

Freddie shouted across to Jamie, "There will be no living with her now!"

Jamie and Jack burst into spontaneous laughter as they followed along. Underneath the dragons flew another set of beings, as a multitude of fairy folk decided they would like to live in Alice's Utopia, too. Beneath the fairies on the ground galloped all manner of creatures, led by centaurs and unicorns.

Alice's little part of the world was about to become much more colourful – and way more interesting when all her guests arrived.

The fifteen-minute flight was nearing its end as the commune loomed before them. Like a group of ace Top Gun pilots, the company of dragons and their precious cargo landed one after another to its side.

Alice lifted her leg over the dragon's neck and slid to the ground carefully cradling her egg, whilst Josie, Freddie, Jack, and Jamie did the same. Jasmine Lester came up to the assembled dragons and welcomed them, as she took Alice by the hand and kissed her cheek.

"That was a very brave thing you did, Alice...you made a decision and acted upon it, with no thought or fear for your own safety," said Jasmine.

"It was the right thing to do. This is a lesson for everyone to live their lives by...never fear your actions, if they are the right ones. Let's all get to know our new friends..." she encouraged.

Alice and her four companions led the dragon leader and the five parents to their watering hole and Alice asked, "Would this be a good place in which to build your nests?"

The dragon leader knew it was, and he instructed, "As you have young, you shall be the first to choose your space. I don't want anyone nearer than fifty claw's distance to the water. That way, the water will always be available to anyone who needs it."

"Thank you for that...shall we let your people nest while we go back and make plans for the future?"

"After you," said the courteous dragon.

As Alice and the dragon returned to the commune, Jasmine once again approached.

"We appear to have more guests!" said Jasmine, pointing excitedly.

Alice looked up into the sky, and saw a multitude of fairy folk...and all around the perimeter of the commune, every conceivable type of animal imaginable.

Will the spring have enough water for all these animals? thought Alice.

*The volcanic water spring is eternal, and will quench the thirst of any who drink from it...*was the resonating answer in Alice's mind.

Alice smiled and raised her arms into the air exultantly, shouting, "Welcome – one and all – come, and join our celebration!"

Keith Johnson and Diane Sanders looked on from the doorway of the watermill, then Diane said, "I have never made nappies that are dragon-sized before..."

Keith replied by saying, "That's ok – I've never made a crib for one either..." Both Keith and Diane laughed heartily as they returned to their respective rooms.

The day wore on, and the dragons settled into their new homes amongst the rocks surrounding the water hole. Everything was now within safe reach, and their children were as safe as the human ones growing within the commune next door.

Sophie Narey had experienced a very busy time writing in her journal, as she was just finishing the part which Delphinium had relayed to her regarding the adventure Alice and her friends had been on. She was about to embark upon covering the preparations which had been made for their arrival when she was met with a bit of confusion.

"I totally understand the story about how Alice and her friends arrived at the dragons' lair, and how they all flew back. The bit I don't get is how the fairy folk knew all this was happening, because Alice told me before she left that it was very much a 'spur-of-the-moment' thing, and she just went with her feelings. So...how did the fairies know to go to the dragons' lair this morning?" said Sophie, with a distinctly questioning look in her eyes.

"I'm sure I don't know..." said Delphinium, looking at the ground, as she hiccupped and appeared quite unsure of herself.

Sophie grinned widely and strolled over to a tree where three fairies were sitting on a branch, swinging their legs, and said, "May I ask, what happens if one of you tells a fib?"

"We can't lie, for if we do, we get uncontrollable hiccups," answered one of the fairies.

"I see..." said Sophie, grinning wider, as she walked back to where she had been sitting. When she sat back down, she watched Delphinium, who was sitting there looking all innocent – but then, 'hic, hic, hic, hic'.

Sophie burst into laughter and said, "Just as I thought...you told them!"

Delphinium looked down and blushed, then owned up, and her hiccups halted.

As Sophie and Delphinium were sitting on the grass laughing, Alice shouted over for Sophie to come and join her and her guests. As Sophie walked over to where they were, her journal appeared in her hand, and her ink-fairy upon her shoulder.

Gathered in a circle were the leaders of all the different animals. Standing opposite to Alice was Gustaf – the magnificent and proud leader of the unicorns – who brought the meeting to a start.

"Hello friends – old and new – here we stand at the dawn of a wonderful new coexistence. The female human sitting opposite me has made all of this possible, and her fellow humans have extended their hands in friendship. As this was the way Mother Nature has ordained it to be, so shall it be. Alice has already stated that none of this belongs to herself or her fellow humans, and has extended an offering of help and sharing towards our brothers and sisters. We, in turn, must now do the same. From this day forward, humans shall walk unhindered wherever they wish, and shall not to be hunted, or harassed in any way. You are all aware of Mother Nature's laws in this respect, and her wishes will be adhered to."

The leader of the centaurs stood and mirrored what Gustaf had said, offering the services of his people towards the coexistence. One by one, each representative of every species on Earth declared their intentions to live in peace. As Sophie was writing all the words of the meeting down, another book appeared on her lap, with the words 'The Animal Covenant' written on its front. Sophie stood and walked into the centre of the circle, and as she did, the area was flooded with a blinding light. At either side of her, two beings of great size and stature materialised. Sophie was scared, but Alice asked her to remain at ease, for she knew that these were friends. As the light dimmed and their vision was restored, Sophie could see that one of the figures was bright, with her own scintillating light emanating from her being...the other was dark, and foreboding. This was the one Sophie feared most as her hands began to tremble, and the book she held started to shake. The dark figure felt her fear, and looked to the Goddess at his side. Mother Nature touched Sophie gently on the shoulder and all her fears disappeared.

The Great Mother began to speak. "Much has been achieved since the dark time of the Apocalypse, and this gathering fills me with delight at the New Beginning which has successfully transpired. All within this circle shall sign this book with the blood of Atkinson." At that point, Delphinium flew up to Atkinson's shoulder and asked, "May I take your blood for Sophie's quill, Great Lord of the Night?"

Atkinson turned his head to the tiny fairy and said, "You have my permission to do so."

Delphinium inserted Sophie's pen's nib into Atkinson's jugular vein, and the inkwell within it filled with the ice-cold blood of the Grim Reaper. Delphinium then returned to Sophie and gave her back the quill.

"My pen...It's so cold...I can hardly hold it."

"Be strong, my dear – if you were not pure of soul, merely holding the quill containing my blood in your hand would have killed you."

Sophie gulped and looked at Mother Nature.

"Sophie, my dear child...be of strong heart, and have no fear. Take the book to everyone sitting in this circle, and pass each one the pen."

Sophie did as she was bid, and took the pen first to Alice. Alice signed her name in Atkinson's blood. An immense feeling of power and love filled her being as she sat back down.

One by one, all the delegates signed the book, and Sophie eventually reached one of the smallest animals there. The pen itself was actually larger than this beast, and when Mother Nature saw who it was, she chuckled and pointed it out to Atkinson, who smiled. Delphinium fluttered down and sat at the side of the animal, explaining that only animals which could harm the human race needed to sign the book.

The proud little animal stood up and said, "I too want to sign the book, as I represent all rodents, and I demand we have the right to do so!"

Atkinson laughed and said, "I am sure the whole of humanity will sleep safer in their beds now that you have signed the book, oh Great Hamster."

The little hamster stuffed another nut into his pouch, and sat back down triumphantly. The hyena at the hamster's side didn't find the hamster amusing at all...nor did he believe in what was being said. Another thing he didn't realise was the reason they were signing with Atkinson's blood...but he soon found out. The very instant the hyena put pen to paper, he was paralysed in a standing position. Atkinson strode over to where he stood, and drew his mighty sword, and the hyena's eyes opened wide in shock and fear as the Reaper approached him. Atkinson drew his sword back further and cut the hyena in two, as its entire species were wiped from existence. As Atkinson passed the pen to the lion sitting next to the empty seat, he looked straight into the lion's eyes, prepared for another challenge. The lion quickly signed his allegiance to the new covenant, as did the rest of the gathered dignitaries, with no further unrest.

As Atkinson returned, Sophie asked him if it was ok for her to record what had just taken place.

"Of course it is, my dear...do explain how ruthless I was," said Atkinson with a grin.

Sophie gulped once more.

Mother Nature stepped forward and said, "What just happened to the hyena and its kind will happen to any of you and yours should you go against this treaty of peace. We have no need to keep an eye on you, as Atkinson's blood will take care of that for us."

As the meeting broke up, some animals decided to move away from the humans' camp, to prevent any of their kind from causing anything like what had just occurred. Others − such as the unicorns, centaurs, and most of the animals that were once extinct – decided to stay with the humans, much to their delight.

The evening sun began to set on a very special day...a day that had seen the mortality rate of the dragons drop tremendously because of the actions of Alice and her friends. A covenant had been signed by all the animals of the forest, paving the way for a safer world for everyone in which to live.

Chapter Thirteen
And on to Tomorrow

om Harper and Steve Bingham's big day had finally arrived, having been summoned by Mother Nature to return to the circle of standing stones they'd visited nine months earlier. At the same time as this meeting was taking place, Tom Harper's sister Linda had gone into labour. The midwife was her heavily-pregnant wife Viktoria Harper, who would be giving birth herself within a day or two.

As the two men entered the stone circle, sitting upon the altar was the Goddess herself, holding a baby...the baby she had promised them at its conception. The child's DNA was comprised of sperm from both men, and an egg from Viktoria Harper. This was truly a baby born of both men, and was indeed their own.

Mother Nature smiled and held out the baby as Steve Bingham took hold of the proffered child. The Goddess placed her arms around both men, and the baby opened her eyes, and saw her parents for the first time. Both men cried, as the emotion of the event was so intense. Tom Harper kissed his tiny new daughter on the forehead, then kissed his lover on the lips, saying, "I love you, Steve."

Steve Bingham wore a beaming smile and answered, "I love you too, Tom."

Just out of view stood the lonely figure of John Smith, who knew that if things had been different, that could have been him standing there with Tom. He thought he might cry – but the emotionless Reaper could not muster a tear as he silently turned away.

"Fleeting moments like this would not make up for an eternity of loss when Tom – and later, the baby – both died, John..." said another pregnant female quietly from behind him.

John Smith turned to see Tamara...who was now sporting a lump containing Atkinson's child.

"I know – I just needed to witness this for some closure. How is your pregnancy coming along?"

"It is coming along fine...only a few more years to go before it's born," laughed Tamara.

"Almost as long as an elephant's pregnancy!"

"Yes – and I'm sure I will be the size of one at the end!" replied Tamara with a giggle.

Tamara placed her arm around John and gave him a smile as the two of them disappeared back to the place from whence they came.

As the two proud fathers returned to the commune, they found Keith Johnson and Diane Sanders had already paid them a visit...a crib, a pile of baby clothes, and nappies were already waiting for them.

Not long after they returned, Alice knocked upon their door.

"Hello, Alice, have you come to see the baby?" asked Tom.

"Of course I have! However, I've also come to let you know you are an uncle as well as a father today...Linda has had her baby!"

Tom looked over at Steve with big eyes, and Steve sighed and said, "Off you go...I can take care of things here until you return...but don't take all day about it!"

Tom ran to his sister's house, where he found Viktoria holding their new son. "Is she ok?" asked an eager Tom.

"Mother and child are absolutely fine. How are things with you?"

"We had a girl!" blurted Tom, as he sat by his sister Linda and held her hand.

"It certainly is a month for babies – what with Alice finally giving birth to the twins, then you and Linda...and very soon me," remarked Viktoria.

"Indeed, it has! Also, many of the women who were pregnant in the first wave of new life are pregnant again!" said Tom.

"I know! Last year has certainly been a busy one for us midwives."

"Yes, it has...and I'm glad to say it will be that way for a long time to come," answered Tom, as his sister awoke and saw him.

"Hello, you – are you a dad yet?" smiled Linda.

"Indeed, I am – and I see you have made me an uncle on the same day! You always did steal my thunder..." quipped Tom as he kissed her.

"Yes, well...that's because I have always been better than you," she said with a smile.

Tom pulled a face.

"What's that face for?" demanded his sister.

"I always look like that when I kiss a girl! Yuk – it's nasty!"

"Shut up! You know you love it, you old queen!"

"Puhlease, girlfriend...dream on! Look after that nephew of mine!" shouted Tom as he was leaving.

"By the way...what did you get?" yelled Linda.

"You are the auntie of a niece...and auntie is quite fitting, considering how you look these days..." Quipped Tom.

Linda threw a pillow at him, then burst into laughter.

Viktoria brought their son and gently handed him to Linda. The baby latched onto her nipple and began to nurse.

"Did you ever think we would be in a situation like this, my love?" smiled Viktoria.

"I love you so much," said Linda.

Away from all the newborn babies at the edge of a field of rye stood Kareem Farmer, who was very proud of his first field of grain, readying Keith Johnson's harvester. Keith had been perfecting this machine alongside working with Jamie Winters on his latest project.

The field was vast, and Kareem had tried to evaluate how much grain he would need to make bread for the humans and all the other species that partook of such food. One such species was the centaurs...and as they were to gain as many bags of flour as they should have need of, they had been helping with the upkeep of the field. Two of the centaurs were required to pull Keith's contraption whilst the humans would load the cut rye onto the backs of others. Keith had also fashioned a simple thrashing machine, which would help move things along at a quicker pace.

Josie Anderson was looking forward to baking bread, as it seemed such a long time since she had baked – or even tasted – bread. All of this depended upon the project Jamie and Freddie were working on, with the help of Keith, Jack, Michael, and Wendy...for at the very far end of the field, high on the hill, stood Jamie's windmill.

Jamie had begun working on the windmill right after finishing the watermill. The windmill was the first building made with wooden planks...as Keith's circular saw had proved an asset, producing as many planks as Jamie had asked for. The construction of the windmill went slowly at first, because the two great stones required for grinding the rye had to be shaped, then fitted into place. Everything else – the lifting gear, the sails, and all of the working components – had given Jamie little in the way of problems, as he had learned first-hand from Master Builders of such mills in the past.

Today was the day that the last part of the mill had been fitted. As everyone from the commune made their way to the rye field, Jamie sent a message to Kareem that he was ready to receive the first batch of rye.

In a joyous mood, Alice's entire brood turned up at the field, ready for their day's work in the sun. A group of centaurs was also in attendance, and Kareem Farmer handed out the duties of the day. The centaurs' main job would involve the pulling of Keith Johnson's harvesting machine, and transporting the cut rye to the thresher. Humans would hand-cut the rye that the machine couldn't reach, operate the thresher, and bag the ears of rye, transporting them – with the help of the centaurs – to Jamie in his windmill.

This was a Red-Letter Day for the commune, as it marked the beginning of their very own agricultural revolution. Kareem had marked out four other fields for growing potatoes, cabbage, carrots, and peas. These four crops would be rotated each year, and fertiliser from the composting toilets would be used to keep the soil high in nutrients. A fifth field had also been prepared, so at the end of each growing season, one field would be at rest. This basic husbandry from pre-Industrial Revolution times was perfect in the New Age of Humankind.

Everyone worked diligently, so it wasn't long before the first sacks of rye were delivered to Jamie at his mill. It seemed as if Mother Nature was working as hard as they were, for a gentle wind was blowing, keeping the workers in the field cool, and the blades on Jamie's windmill turning.

Back at the commune, Josie anxiously awaited the first batch of flour. She had already prepared her yeast, utilising potatoes which grew naturally all around the commune. The past year had been a good one for Josie and Kareem, because he had discovered so many things that she could use. For instance, his identification of sugarcane had made Josie very happy indeed...not just as a sweetener, but as an ingredient facilitating making the yeast she needed for the bread she would bake. All of the vegetables and herbs Kareem had discovered, he had harvested seeds from, for when his crop rotation scheme came into play. In fact, since Alice had freed Kareem to concentrate solely on his botany, he had become a Miracle Worker, finding new foods on a daily basis for Josie to add to her ever-changing menu. That day's work in the field gave Kareem a great sense of satisfaction, reinforcing Alice's decision to make him her botanist.

The day moved on, and after one or two false starts, Jamie had the intricate workings of his new windmill doing what they were supposed to do – producing flour. The flour was of fine-grade – perfect for Josie's baking. By the end of the day the rye field was empty, the grain store was full, the straw was stacked and under cover, and the windmill was working at optimal performance. A very-dusty Jamie closed the mill for the night and returned to the commune, where he tried – for the first time in ages, a slice of bread and butter. The bread had been made with flour from his very own mill, and the butter from the dairy cows who wandered up to the pasture twice a day to be milked. Jamie put his tired feet up as he finished the most delicious slice of bread he'd ever eaten in his life, then fell fast asleep.

The harvest was in and safe from the elements as Autumn donned her gown. The approaching winter would be the first one in which the commune was totally self-sufficient. There was enough food, and plenty of readily-available running water and fuel. Alice completed her check of the three store rooms and knew she had enough of everything she needed, plus the ability to help any other species that struggled during the winter. Every species now lived in peaceful harmony, none coveting what another had. Alice smiled to herself as she closed the door behind her, returning to her log cabin, her husband Freddie, and their two children, Doris and Glenda.

Many years later, the oldest couple within the commune were very proud of their two children. The thought of Alice taking over the family haulage business had long since dissipated from the memories of Alfred and Amanda Winters. The pride they had in their daughter Alice was immense. She had – with the help of a few others – saved the world's population, and through her link with Mother Nature given the people of the New World everything they needed to flourish. Their son Jamie was the one who led the team of New World civil engineers, which had begun their very own Industrial Revolution, and partially-mechanised the commune. Their grandchildren were following in their mother's footsteps, and were now helping Alice run communes all over the world.

Alice's parents could not understand why she looked just as she had all those years ago when they'd first emerged from the safety shelter; both her children and her brother now looked older than she. That, of course, was a secret between Alice, Mother Nature, and Atkinson.

50 years had passed since Alice led 49 people from their shelter into the New World. A lot of things had changed in that time, but there was always one constant – and that constant was Alice Winters-Chambers. There were two other constants, remaining unseen...one was Mother Nature, who had provided life and sustenance for the past 50 years. The other constant was Atkinson...and after his fifty-year break, he strode back into the Realm of Death in his Alpha Reaper armour with his great sword in his hand, as two mortal cords fell from the ceiling. The Grim Reaper took hold of Alfred and Amanda Winters' cords, made a loop in them and ran his blade through.

On the Plane of Existence. The first two deaths of the New World took place, and the Reaper was back in Administration. The post-apocalyptical people had been gifted new life by Mother Nature...but as Atkinson could only deal death, he granted Humanity absolution, as he guided its first two departed souls to a new life.

And what of Tamara and Atkinson's son...of Sarah, Gavin, and Paladin...of John Smith...of Paul and Dixie Johnson, and their two children? What of all the human adventures taking place in a New World of magic and peace amongst the unicorns and centaurs?

One day, I will answer these questions...

but for now, this is

The End

JOHN PAUL BERNETT

List of Characters in The Reaper Series

Book One	Atkinson's Administration
Book Two	Atkinson's Armageddon
Book Three	Atkinson's Adversary
Book Four	Atkinson's Apprentice
Book Five	Atkinson's Apocalypse
Book Six	Atkinson's Absolution

Atkinson – The Alpha Reaper

(Based on John Paul Bernett)

Atkinson Senior is the God of Death...The Alpha Reaper. He has delivered Death to every dominant species this world has ever known, and has been doing this job since Life itself began. He was once a great Reaper, but now has lost all interest in the current dominant species, and wants to end their existence. He is, quite simply, the strongest entity upon the planet...and wields powers beyond human thought. His domain is The Other Realm, where he resides as The Scribe, as he has long since given up his role as The Reaper. To this end, he introduced his son – Atkinson Junior – to take over his Administrations, and to share the reaping with Dewhirst. As each Administration passes, he grows ever-more disgruntled with the entire circle of Death and Life, and believes it is time for a different dominant species. He hates the human race with a passion, and would see it extinct, as the dinosaurs he tired of long ago.

Dewhirst – The Eternal Scribe

(Based on Keith Johnson)

Dewhirst has been the work partner of Atkinson ever since time began. As Atkinson reaped the soul, Dewhirst would quill the name into the Great Book of Existence. As the workload increased, Dewhirst also began to reap, and the two would take it in turns in twenty-five-year Administrations as The Reaper. During the last two millennia, Dewhirst has become more and more active…and during the 16th century, he made a permanent office upon the Plane of Existence, naming it Atkinson, Atkinson & Dewhirst. This is the accountancy front which hides what its inhabitants really do…and the business is still housed within that very same building. Dewhirst, however, grows weary…and unlike his counterpart, looks forward to The Prophecy, which states that one day, they shall be replaced. Again – unlike his counterpart Atkinson – he has a fondness for humans, as he can see their potential. He also knows the human race won't just 'lie down and die' merely because Atkinson wills it to be.

Atkinson Junior – a.k.a. Death

(Based on Lee Coates)

Atkinson Junior is the Fourth Rider of the Apocalypse; he is Death...The Grim Reaper. He is the son of an ancient God, and wields similar powers. He has worked with Atkinson – his father – and Dewhirst the Scribe for countless millennia. It is his greatest wish to change the system, and become The Alpha Reaper. When in Administration, he resides upon The Plane of Existence within the offices of Atkinson, Atkinson & Dewhirst in the guise of an accountant...but he does his true work in the Realm of Death, where he cuts the mortal cords of humans whose life numbers have reached their end. He severs their mortal cord which links them from the Plane of Existence to the Realm of Death, thus ending that particular human's life. How the human dies is of no interest to him...he only cares about their life number...the very last digit.

Sarah/Slabgirl – a.k.a. War

(Based on Sarah Fae Graham)

Sarah is the War Warrior of the Apocalypse when in a different realm. On the Plane of Existence, she is the Gothic 'Slabgirl', as she is known to her friends. These two beings could not be further apart, because Slabgirl is a loveable, dippy, awkward and bumbling girl who is always dropping things, and her behaviour leaves a lot to be desired. Slabgirl was saved from an abusive home life by her boss (and soon-to-be-husband), and became a college student. She works at the mortuary, where she met Gavin Jackson. She is the bane of Tom Harper's (the mortuary assistant) life.

Sarah the Warrior, on the other hand, is a cold-hearted killer who has been bested by no-one, ever...not even Atkinson. She became the deadliest force on the planet after giving birth to Paladin in the Realm of Nature. She is held in high regard by both Mother Nature and Atkinson. One other thing about this Warrior...she is the daughter of Dewhirst. Of all the Apocalyptical Horse-Riders,

fear this one the most.

Aquallia – a.k.a. Famine

(Based on Samantha Webster)

The Kraken is not a giant squid...she is a beautiful mermaid...beautifully deadly, that is. Whenever Mother Nature decides it is time for a cleansing, Aquallia is who she calls upon. She is the Bringer of the Tsunami...the Destroyer of Continents. To see her is to die. Her song...although the sweetest sound you will ever hear, is also the last sound you will ever hear. A whole fleet of warships is no match for her might. Once the Kraken is invoked, the End is near. Once summoned, she lives for 16 weeks as a sweet Merchild...but come the end of her 16th week, all Hell breaks loose, and any soul at sea will be lost to the ocean. She has no compassion...she has no predators. Her only role is to do Mother Nature's and Atkinson's bidding, and deliver Death from the oceans of the world. As far as marine life is concerned, she is its Goddess...a Goddess not to be angered.

Paladin – a.k.a. Pestilence

(Based on Hunter Tate)

Paladin is the offspring of Sarah and The Sentinel...a product of God-like form created by Mother Nature herself. A dual purpose has he...to destroy, and to rebuild. Paladin is The Apprentice to Atkinson when it comes to Death...but in Life, he is the Guiding Light of Nature. He is Mother Nature's right hand on the Plane of Existence during the Apocalypse.

He is the Bringer of Hope...the Promised One, who can mend Humanity. A simple touch of his hand can relieve a lifetime's worth of anguish...but should you not heed his words, your death will mean nothing to him, as he passes over to his next assignment. Paladin has a companion – a shape-shifting Wood Nymph from the Realm of Nature called Juliantrium...and together, they are formidable. Juliantrium is his every mode of transport, and will fulfil his every request. Heed this particular Horse-Rider of the Apocalypse's words...they may give you a new way of thinking; on the other hand, ignore them...at your peril.

John Smith – Surrogate & Reaper

(Based on John Mac McCormick)

John Smith is the mild-mannered accountant who works at Atkinson, Atkinson & Dewhirst, the local accountancy firm. His job is as strange as the company he works for, because he is the Surrogate for a God...a God of Death. He is one of the main characters in The Reaper Series, and his development begins in Book I, with him going from strength to strength as the story unfolds. He works in the Realm of Death as The Grim Reaper when in Administration...but when on the Plane of Existence, he returns to a loveable, tea-drinking accountant. He has been a Surrogate to Atkinson Junior since the Middle Ages...but now, as the 21st century dawns, he finds his own way, as promotion makes his role as Surrogate redundant. He discovers a fulfilling existence, and for the first time in his life has friends...one of which becomes very special to him.

Tamara – The List-Maker

(Based on Donna Dickinson)

Tamara is the legendary List-Maker and Warrior...her job is to psychically receive the names of the soon-to-be departed, placing them upon the Reaper's Death List. She is the epitome of beauty and elegance. Don't get on the wrong side of this Immortal being, because her beauty is only surpassed by her strength. She is also the lover of Atkinson Junior...but has a fondness for human pleasures, as well...be they male or female. She is the daughter of Dewhirst, and sister of Sarah...a very high-ranking official within the Reaper System. One of her roles is to protect Atkinson Junior...and she has fought many a battle at his side, never being bested. Her demeanour within the company on the Plane of Existence is that of a personal assistant...but she is much more than that, because if she did not write the lists, the Reaper System would fail. She is the original List-Maker, and as such, has sat across from the Reaper in Administration well before Humanity dominated the planet. She has written the name of every single human being that has ever walked upon the Plane of Existence...she is the one and only Tamara.

Mr. Braithwaite – Administrator

(Based on our wonderful old friend Albert)

Mr. Braithwaite appears to be an octogenarian...but don't let his trembling hands and aged demeanour fool you...he is, in fact, the most powerful Elemental from the Other Realm. He works for Dewhirst, and is in charge of the Ledger Department. He holds an important position, as the commodity he deals in is Life itself. He has fulfilled this role as long as Atkinson and Dewhirst have wielded the mighty Sword of Death, and his bookwork on the Plane of Existence must match the Scribe's Great Book of Souls in the Other Realm. There can be no clerical errors within this firm. Whenever anything needs doing within the old Tudor building, Mr. Braithwaite oversees the work, and what he says goes. Even Atkinson cannot interfere with Mr. Braithwaite's bookwork. He may appear old and infirm, but there is much more to this Office Administrator than meets the eye, as his hands can swiftly pass from his walking stick to a sword.

Paul Johnson – Detective Inspector

(Based on Mark Valentine)

Paul Johnson was the Detective Inspector who worked for Chief Inspector Jack Thompson. He then became Chief Inspector himself as a result of his superior's death. Fate had other plans for Paul Johnson – or rather, Atkinson did – after an incident beyond his control made it necessary that he take over from the popular Chief Inspector. He excelled during and after the initial devastation that nearly wrecked the entire city, working tirelessly during the following year to rebuild confidence in the police force and community alike. He was decorated for bringing law and order back to the streets. Destined to climb the promotional ladder as far as he should wish, the future of the new Chief Inspector looked rosy to all but himself...he struggled having the knowledge of what the local firm of accountants did...and this knowledge took its toll upon him. In a moment of weakness, he decides he can go on no longer...however, his intention to end it all is halted by John Smith, who offers him a different lifestyle and new career within Atkinson, Dewhirst & Smith.

Gavin Jackson – Coroner/Sentinel

(Based on Gavin Johnson)

Doctor Gavin Jackson is the new wiz-kid in town and has taken over Dr. Grayson as the town's coroner. In his new situation, he has joined a small team...his assistant Dr. Tom Harper, and the crazy Goth-child, Slabgirl. Slabgirl is the mortuary's 'Gopher'...she makes the tea, washes the tables down, and annoys Tom. Gavin has a new way of working that Tom Harper admires. He also falls in love, which totally bewilders Tom. Gavin also has a supernatural life...he is the mighty Sentinel...and this particular Sentinel, no-one passes. He is the father of Paladin, and husband to the greatest supernatural Warrior that has ever existed. The flip-side of that coin means he is also married to the biggest scatterbrain on the planet. He hails from aristocracy, but has the ability to mix with anyone. He drives a classic Jaguar, and always dresses to impress.

Dixie Atkinson – Elemental Warrior

(Based on Clare Gollop)

Dixie rises from a lowly Elemental to one of Atkinson's bravest Warriors. We first meet her as she is introduced as Paul Johnson's travelling companion. It soon becomes clear that there is something special about this Elemental. Her role is to protect and serve Paul, and to keep him happy as he begins his quest – as predicted in The Great Prophecy. When she sees the legendary List-Maker, Tamara, she aspires to be just like her. Her goal is to be eternally matched with Paul Johnson, as she falls in love with him, and the ex-Chief Inspector succumbs to her charms. She displays how powerful and useful she can be when she is sent by Atkinson to the Dark Realm to help his favourite Warriors. Her bravery wins Tamara and Atkinson over as they accept her into the firm, and grant her Immortality. She never forgets where she came from, but will always remember the day Tamara pointed her finger and told her what her new job was to be. Dixie's Plane of

Existence demeanour is a young and attractive secretary who is unworldly and shy...in different realms, she is a ruthless Warrior.

Jeff Clarke – Young Reporter

(Based on Josh Hughes)

Jeff Clarke was sent to a police station to observe how a press conference proceeds when he stumbled upon something that could end the world. He learned a lot that night, as he watched an old newsman put the police through their paces. He made it his intention to team up with that newsman (Sid Jenkins), and together they reopen an old story from almost a quarter of a century ago. As he is working on said story, he suddenly finds himself alone, with all the evidence to write the 'story of stories'. Unfortunately, before he could write it, fate changes the playing field. His life is turned upside-down as a career at Atkinson, Dewhirst & Smith looms, and the young reporter needs to grow up – fast. As he begins this new life, there are many things from his old life he misses...such as his work colleagues, friends and family...but Jeff Clarke knows that what he must do has to be done... and only he can do it.

Juliantrium – Shape-Shifting Wood Nymph

(Based on Lynette Ong)

Juliantrium hails from the Realm of Nature. She is a Shape-Shifting Wood Nymph – the daughter and favourite of Mother Nature – and has an extremely-powerful brother. Mother Nature pairs her with Paladin, and together they make a formidable team. Her shape-shifting abilities take her from a unicorn to a Harley-Davidson motorbike...from a helicopter to a small person. Her ability to change is boundless...her strength, legendary. Her ability to protect Paladin is never in question...she is a beautiful and powerful Pixie, and Mother Nature's strength flows through her veins. As a Wood Nymph, she is a Muse of Love; as a Warrior, Sarah is the only one who is stronger. This entity is the stuff dreams are made of...and when on the Plane of Existence, as well as protecting Paladin and her sisters, she is a protector of animals.

Sophie Neary – New World Journal-Keeper

(Based on Sophie Neary)

Sophie Neary is the New World's event-recorder. She enters the story in Book 5, and is very prominent in Book 6. Sophie is a young lady who is very well-read, intelligent and attractive. She was on holiday in Ireland when the Apocalypse struck, and discovered cast adrift with two other ladies after it had passed. She was saved by one of Atkinson's Warriors, and brought back to a cave for shelter, where she met her old school-friend Slabgirl. Sophie was amazed to see her friend in the guise of Sarah the Warrior, and at Sarah's request, Dewhirst gave her the position at the beginning of the New World Order as the person who would pen all the activities of Humanity as it started anew. After she leaves the cave with her new friends, she meets up with an enchanted fairy, and Alice Winters-Chambers, and begins documenting the events taking place in the New World.

Alice Winters-Chambers – Mother Nature's Human Vessel

(Based on Kelly Coates)

Alicia Winters, as she was first known, appears in the prequel to The Reaper Series, and was a spoiled bitch of a woman...rich beyond measure, with a disregard for basically everything. In a Switch in Time – the first prequel to The Reaper Series – Alicia was taken back in time by Mother Nature as an experiment, to see if Humankind could change for the better. The experiment was successful, and Alicia Winters changed her ways, becoming an upstanding citizen...she in fact did far better than Mother Nature could have hoped. When she returned to her own time, she took on the name of 'Alice', and married Freddie Chambers. Alice took over the family business, and began using the profits to house homeless young people on the streets of Leeds. This endeavour led to a meeting with Paladin. Paladin liked how she did business, and a meeting was arranged with Mother Nature herself. The outcome of that meeting was that Alice Winters-Chambers would run Nature Industries, and become Mother Nature's Earth-bound presence. She was responsible for the construction of every shelter which saved Humankind from extinction, and the one who guided the entire planet of survivors into the New Dawn of Humanity.

Jack Thompson – Chief Inspector

(Based on Ian Warrington)

Chief Inspector Jack Thompson is of the old school of police work...find the proof, bag the evidence, and get every 'I' dotted and all the 'Ts' crossed before making an arrest. He is one of the most-decorated police officers in the North of England. His thirty-year career is unblemished – his conviction rate second-to-none in the entire country. He rose to Chief Inspector quite early in his career, but didn't want to progress higher, as a desk job was definitely not for him. He never used methods of entrapment, or any process of criminal detection that wasn't in the manuals. He is a man of impeccable dress-sense and manners, always doing the right thing. He does, however, struggle adjusting to the 'new kids on the block' taking over from his old friends. New ideas don't rest easy with him, as we discover when he first meets Gavin Jackson in Book I. As an instructor, he made Detective Inspector Paul Johnson the police officer that he became.

Glenn Simpson – Desk Sergeant

(Based on our dear friend Glenn Simpson)

Desk Sergeant Glenn Simpson is the stalwart of the police station. He was a young bobby on the beat with P.C. Jack Thompson when a spate of murders rocked the community twenty-two years earlier, and has been at the police station ever since. During the devastation at the turn of the twenty-first century, he almost lost his life, and was instrumental in evacuating the old police station before it was destroyed. He took the loss of Chief Inspector Jack Thompson badly, as they were old friends. It was Sergeant Simpson who saved Superintendent Viktoria Malik by evacuating her safely from the station following Chief Inspector Crawshaw's moment of madness...and indirectly, he became the matchmaker for his Superintendent and Police Officer Linda Harper. This Desk Sergeant tolerates no nonsense, and everything must be written down properly. Unrest is not allowed when he is on duty, and respect is demanded from every rank...he is a multi-decorated and respected officer of the law.

Simone Baudelaire – Team Leader

(Based on Simone Baudelaire)

Simone has always been a Child of the Night. She loves rainy days, and dresses in Gothic clothing. She – like many others – finds herself drawn to one of Nature Industries' protection shelters, and just like people from all over the world who are lucky enough to find one of these shelters, she sits down and quietly takes her place. Unbeknownst to her, Mother Nature has chosen her as the safety shelter's Team Leader...she discovers this fact when a police officer asks her what to do after an old lady with white hair tells him Simone is in charge...the very same old lady that Simone has been dreaming about her whole life. Her new role becomes the safe-keeping of the Scottish shelter inhabitants, and to assist them in identifying their unique duties for which they have been spared to perform.

Jed Jeffries – NASA Flight Director

(Based on Kevin Moyles)

Jed Jeffries – or 'JJ', as he is known to his controllers – has been a Flight Director at NASA for many years. He began his career as an apprentice at the end of the Apollo missions, and has been there ever since. He is first called upon in Atkinson's Armageddon, where he heads a team at Mission Control to ease the world's worries when an asteroid gets knocked out of its normal orbit and is set upon a collision course with the Earth. Then – in Atkinson's Apocalypse – he and his team are again called upon to perform several missions simultaneously, to aid the planet's ozone problem. They do not know it, but this is a joint effort with Mother Nature herself. NASA, however, has a problem...at the same time the ozone-saving mission meets a successful end, Jed Jeffries and his team of controllers are alerted to a new problem at the International Space Station...the Space Station and all the planets' artificial satellites are losing their orbits. This problem is the strangest occurrence NASA has ever come across since it took its first tentative steps towards the stars.

Viktoria Malik – Chief Superintendent

(Based on Viktoria Malik)

Chief Superintendent Viktoria Malik is a tough, no-nonsense type of person...she works in a male-dominated world...but no man dominates this police officer; many have tried, and all have failed. She climbed the ladder the hard way – she is a cop through-and-through, and rules the police station with an iron fist. She has worked tirelessly to remove any form of sexism, racism and homophobia from her part of the police force. She leads by example, and never asks one of her officers to do anything that she hasn't already done many times herself. She is living proof that women can do anything a man can within the police force, and has risen high up the promotional ladder. Like Police Officer Linda Harper, she has recently 'come out', and let her sexuality be known...to find her 'little secret' really wasn't a secret after all. She has faced death many times...but most recently at the hands of the lunatic Chief Inspector Crawshaw.

Linda Harper – Police Officer

(Based on Tracy Jones)

Police Officer Linda Harper's career has been eventful – and flawless – but something has always stopped her from pushing for a promotion. After being noticed repeatedly by her superiors for her excellent work, and finding her Chief Superintendent was indeed carrying the same secret, she decides to come out and push for a promotion for C.I.D. The information about her sexuality has not altered any of her colleagues' opinions of her...she is a damn fine cop, and has the respect of all who know her. She is good in any situation...from showing an elderly lady where the supermarket is, to a response to an armed robbery. It was her quick response that enabled Chief Superintendent Viktoria Malik to escape the madman Chief Inspector Crawshaw. She impressed her Chief Superintendent in more than just her police work...so much so that they decide to marry. When not in uniform, Linda is a Goth, and has similar tastes in music to Viktoria and Slabgirl. She is the sister of Dr. Tom Harper, the mortuary assistant.

Sid Jenkins – Journalist

(Based on Stephen Johnson)

Sid Jenkins has tried to 'get the scoop' on Atkinson for over a quarter of a century...many times nearly putting all the pieces of the story together, but never quite managing it...until now, that is. The new spate of murders match perfectly with the ones from twenty-two years earlier...and this time, he really is onto something as he teams up with the young, inexperienced but hard-working Jeff Clarke. Sid is from the old school of Journalism, and doesn't quite understand some of Jeff's new-fangled ideas. He has worked at the newspaper as long as its current editor, Donald Steele...but prefers to stay as he is rather than climb the editorial ladder. Also, he doesn't have the connections in Fleet Street that his editor has to reach where he has risen to. Singular-minded with a nose for a good story, but never quite making the broad sheets, he finally comes face to face with Atkinson...which doesn't end well for Sid... nor Atkinson, for that matter.

William Crawshaw – Chief Inspector

(Based on Tony Batley)

Chief Inspector Crawshaw took over the police station on Park Road from Chief Inspector Paul Johnson. His reign at Park Road sparks the worst time that the place has ever witnessed, as far as morale is considered. Crawshaw is the most egotistical, sexist, racist, corrupt police officer the force has ever known...he rose through the ranks through bribery and deception. This man has no respect for anyone, or anything. He is, in fact, worse than many of the people he himself has put behind bars. It is his lack of empathy and low standing in regards to decency that make him prey to dark forces from an even darker realm. This man will stop at nothing to get where he wants to be – and that becomes his eventual downfall, as he is easily taken over by the Dark Realm. He slips from bad cop to demonically-possessed puppet...where he goes, no-one would want to tread; his soul is lost, and his humanity bereft. This man is the worst kind of human there is, my wonderful friend, Tony however, is the nicest guy you will ever meet.

Harriette Jackson

(Based on Deborah Priestley)

Harriette Jackson is the Lady of the Manor, and Chair-Person of the Allerton-Chapel branch of the Women's Institute. She keeps her home running smoothly with the help of her butler Jarvis, cook Mrs. Jarvis, and chambermaid Alice Jarvis. She is the daughter of an aristocrat – and along with husband Donald, is rich beyond belief. She doesn't suffer fools, but once she warms to someone, that someone's life changes forever. She is very protective of her family...especially her only son and heir, Dr. Gavin Jackson, Coroner, who she is very proud of...but cannot understand why he chose Pathology rather than medicine. In her opinion, he could have been anything she wanted him to be. She is the epitome of elegance, style and grace. Her garden parties are the stuff of upper-class legend. Ascot, Wimbledon, and the Varsity Boat Race are all on this socialite's calendar...none of which would impress her new daughter-in-law.

Donald Jackson

(Based on Bernard Smith)

Donald Jackson is an upper-class gentleman who loves motor-racing, horse-racing, and owns a private box at his favourite football club, Leeds United. Many a business deal has been finalized whilst watching the Whites play. He is an eccentric with Irish roots. He in fact met his wife Harriette whilst on a fishing trip to Southern Ireland. He has a love of classic sports cars, and owns quite a few, which are stored in his – as he calls it – 'small garage'. He has reached a stage in his life where he can relax, and find different ways to avoid getting under Harriette's feet. He adores fine brandy...and much to Harriette's discontent, has begun wearing a monocle. He purchased his son Gavin a classic Jaguar for his 21st birthday...but he himself drives an Aston-Martin. The new fascination in his life is his wonderfully-dippy daughter-in-law, whom he encourages to do things around the house that he himself is no longer able to do...like sliding down huge banisters. Harriette, of course, heartily discourages such raucous behaviour.

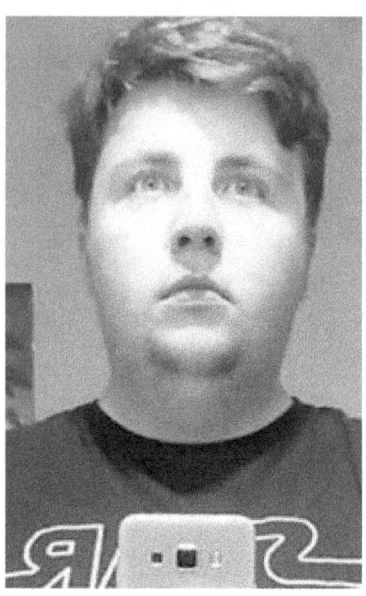

Matthew Hamilton – Hypnotist

(Based on Joseph Williams)

Matthew Hamilton – or Matt, to his friends – is a friend of Jeff Clarke's. He was instrumental in the police enquiries on the murders at John Smith's apartment, and it was his hypnotic skills which sped up their investigation, bringing Book I – Atkinson's Administration – to its conclusion. Matt becomes friends with John Smith, and shows him there is much more to life than accountancy. John Smith indeed flourishes with this new friendship. Without Matt, Chief Inspector Paul Johnson would never have realised the importance of John Smith to the investigation...and this would have been tragic for the world as a whole. He was one of the main players in Atkinson's game of Armageddon...and he paid the ultimate price for trying to stop Atkinson's plans. Indeed, if Matt hadn't put John under hypnosis, the world as we know it would have ended at the turn of the 21st century.

Cindy – Girlfriend of Jeff Clarke

(Based on Beth Smith)

Cindy is the loving girlfriend of Jeff Clarke...they fell in love with one another in school, and have been a couple ever since. She works as a cafeteria assistant in the canteen at the newspaper building. Unlike most of the young ladies which work there, she isn't frightened of the thunderous editor. She is a trainee cook, and hopes one day to become a chef. Cindy loves her job, as it means she can regularly see Jeff, as he works there, too. Young love can have its tragedies...and this Romeo and Juliet are no exception. Whenever they can be, they are together, and never grow tired of each other's company. A disaster alters Cindy's life forever...and the aftermath of what happens saddens everyone. However, all is not what it seems, as she proves love can traverse even the most difficult of situations. True love, or divine intervention? All will be revealed in Book II, Atkinson's Armageddon.

Jasmine Lester

(Based on Imani Brown)

Jasmine appeared in Atkinson's Armageddon as an all-seeing patient in a hospital that John Smith visited. She recognized him as the Reaper, but she – or indeed, Smith – didn't know he'd been sent there to mark her for Mother Nature. She reappears in Atkinson's Apocalypse, Book 5...but she comes into her own in Book 6 – Atkinson's Absolution – becoming Alice Winters-Chambers' second-in-command. She is a strong woman who has brought up two children, both of whom which have excelled. Her son and daughter also prove invaluable to Alice with their skills in leadership and people management...and, in her son's case, engineering. Jasmine's drive and motivation are skills that enable Alice to traverse the planet helping others, knowing the hard work will still continue in her absence.

Mina Lester

(Based on Natania Flavius)

Mina – the daughter of Jasmine Lester – is a trained Psychologist. She is also a lady who can inspire people to greatness...she is one of those who can motivate others to believe in themselves. Like her mother, she is a natural-born leader. Mina admires her mother for the way she single-handedly brought her and her brother up, working long hours to pay for her children to attend university. In return, Mina excelled in all of her subjects, gaining an honour's degree in Psychology. She has a wonderful relationship with her brother Michael, who – like her – was a high-achiever at his university. Mina takes on a new role after the Apocalypse reduces the world's population dramatically, as good leaders are hard to come by. She becomes influential during Book 6, Atkinson's Absolution, as she finds her new life and purpose very rewarding.

Jack Howard – Meteorologist

(Based on Jack Howard)

Mr. Howard is the head of Britain's Meteorology Department. His is the last word when it comes to the weather. He is the youngest person ever to be elevated to this esteemed position, and also the smartest – being over-qualified. He is a man of high morals who believes in equality in all things. When not at the MET office, he loves listening to music, and owns a vast record collection. Jack frequents Goth clubs up and down the country, even deejaying from time to time. He is not a stiff-collared intellectual, and knows how to have fun. He also has a passion for photography. Jack Howard briefly enters the story during Book 5, Atkinson's Apocalypse. People like Mr. Howard are few and far between, and will be needed after the Apocalypse hits, when his greatest potential is finally realized.

Alice Jarvis – Chambermaid

(Based on Laura Louise Hullah)

Alice is the daughter of Mr. and Mrs. Jarvis, her father being the Jackson's butler. She has spent her whole life living alongside the Jacksons, as her mother and father have been in their employ for over 30 years. She loves her life, and it is very different to living in service in the old days. Alice's best friend whilst growing up was Gavin Jackson...he was like an older brother to her instead of a master. Gavin took her everywhere with him up until leaving for university. When Sarah comes along, Alice gains a new friend, and the two girls begin to share adventures together. She is very industrious at her work, and because of this, she receives the opportunity to run a household for Gavin and Sarah...which, of course, elevates her status to that of her father. She misses her family and the Jacksons terribly, but loves her new life with Gavin and Sarah. Her father is very proud of her achievements.

Wendy Walters – Team Leader

(Based on Wendy 'Woo' Walters)

Wendy Walters was working in England... but on a week's holiday, when the Apocalypse struck, she found herself walking into one of Alice Winters-Chambers' safety shelters back in her beloved Wales. There she stayed until she was informed by Mother Nature that her new role in life was to look after the 49 Welsh people that she was sharing the shelter with. It is unknown why Mother Nature chose her...maybe it was because she was such a strong woman...maybe because of her nursing background. Whatever the reason, Mother Nature could not have chosen a better person for the job. Wendy's Welsh passion shines in Books 5 & 6, as she leads her wards across the Pennines to meet with her Scottish and English counterparts. Wendy teams up with Alice Winters-Chambers, and the two ladies become good friends.

Erin Adams – Librarian

(Based on Erin Adams)

Erin Adams was a librarian before the Apocalypse hit...a shy, retiring bookworm with a passion for anything literary. She had read the classics, but had a love for horror...especially the work of Mr. King. Her day-to-day life was one of a semi-reclusive spinster; it had been three years since her life had had any love interest. Erin often dreamed of being in a different place, just like the ones from the books she read. Little did she know that Fate was about to make this dream a reality. One day whilst walking home from work, she noticed a building which had been renovated over the previous few weeks was now open to the public. She went inside, and decided to stay for a while. The doors of the building closed, and the Apocalypse hit the planet. While she sat there, perfectly at ease within her safety shelter, Mother Nature placed her hand upon Erin's tummy. When Erin left the shelter, she discovered that somehow, she was pregnant...destined to give birth to the first child born in the New World. Sophie Neary – the Keeper of the New History of the World – wrote Erin's name into the book as Humanity's first mother.

Michael Lester

(Based on Rashad Chef Augustus Farmer)

Michael Lester is the son of Jasmine Lester, and brother to Mina. He is a genius academically, but he is also an amateur engineer. He is a multi-skilled man who can turn his hands to anything. His character enters the story in Book 5, Atkinson's Apocalypse...but he comes into his own in Book 6, Atkinson's Absolution. He soon teams up with Jamie and Freddie Winters and Jack Howard, and they become a formidable team in the rebuilding process that is taking place in what used to be Great Britain. Michael is a quick thinker and brilliant teacher, as he shares his extensive building knowledge with the people of the New Age of Humanity. He is a valued member of Alice Winters-Chambers' team of four civil engineers. His ability to build – and teach others, he finds – becomes much more important than his scientific knowledge.

Mia – Queen of the Unicorns

(Based on Mia Catherine Joseph)

The Unicorn Queen is one of Mother Nature's most trusted Ethereal beings. She stands nine feet tall, and is one of the strongest powers within Nature's Realm. She hails from a long-extinct species of animal...she is, in fact, a unicorn...but in human form. She has the ability to change back into her unicorn self, and does so whenever she needs to visit the Valley of the Extinct within the Realm of Nature. She wields a great power...and that power is Animal Communication. Mia has the ability to enable any species of animal the ability to converse with and understand any other species upon the planet. This special power Mia wields has long-since left the Earth – with the unicorns – because Mother Nature decreed Humanity undeserving of such a gift after they

188

began to hunt this most sacred of beasts. Mia leads the animals back onto the Plane of Existence one full year after Humanity's cull...and only humans with no desire for hunting or domination are left. The New Humanity begins their lives with the promise of never killing again...but should it ever occur, they will answer to Mia – Queen of the Unicorns.

Kareem Farmer – Botanist

(Based on Kareem Farmer)

He is, by trade, an Architect from North Wales...but like so many who were saved from the Apocalypse, he has many other skills. He is, in fact, a botanist...but lost interest when the world's governments began replacing organic fertilisers with non-organic materials. He hated the use of pesticides, and created an organic way of controlling pests without damaging the pollinators, or having the need of GM crops. He had worked five years on this botany project when, once finished, he approached the Agriculture Minister with his findings. Unfortunately, everything used the process was readily available, so no multinational company could profit from his idea. Because of this, the government shelved it, making it impossible for him to carry on...this was the reason he returned to being an Architect within a small Welsh firm. He never recovered from the aforesaid events...but Mother Nature asks him to try again.

Josie Anderson – New World Chef

(Based on Josie Smith)

Josie Anderson's heroic journey to safety during the Apocalypse – along with her husband Keith and their two children – is how she enters the story. She and her husband's parental skills help a group of young people whilst they are stuck within a cave for a month when the Apocalypse strikes. Josie has many skills...one of which is cooking, as she is a chef by trade. When the first opportunity arises for a chef to take on the nourishment of all survivors, Josie stands and offers herself for the job. She turns out to be the perfect choice, as for many years she had worked with seasonal vegetables, and used nuts as a main protein source. The entire Anderson family was spared so that Josie could be delivered to the cave which saved her life. While her family would be useful within the New World (her husband being a manual worker and her children of fertile years), she was the one Mother Nature wished for, purely to fulfil the important role as Head Chef to the hungry folks of the New World.

Freddie Chambers

(Based on Kevin Pratchett)

Freddie Chambers is the lifelong friend of Jamie Winters. They have been through many adventures together – such as backpacking around the world – whilst still in their teens. The strangest thing he ever did for Jamie was look after two Victorian siblings, when Alicia and Jamie Winters experienced their Switch in Time. His task was trying to prevent the siblings from discovering anything about the future that they'd found themselves in. This didn't turn out quite as planned, as he failed grimly, even falling in love with the young woman entrusted to his care. His passion is steam power...and together with Jamie, he is restoring a preserved railway. In the strangest turn of events, he marries a woman that – up until Jamie and his sister return from the Victorian era – he hated with a passion; that woman was none other than Alicia Winters, who was destined to become Alice Winters-Chambers. This character appears in all three prequels, plus Books 5 & 6 of The Reaper Series.

Diane Sanders – Seamstress

(Based on Diane Sanders)

The term 'seamstress' hardly befits what this smart lady is capable of...she can card and spin wool into yarn then weave said yarn...anything using needles can be fashioned by her. When the first babies begin being born into the New World, Diane provides every family with clothing and nappies, beginning an exchange system, as the clothes are made to fit babies from 0 to 3 months. After this time, the families return the clothing in exchange for ones to fit the following 3 months, and so on. It isn't too long before she has a complete stock of children's clothing, all of which is reusable for the next generation to be born. She partners with Keith Johnson – the commune's carpenter – and together, they share the watermill built by Jamie Winters' team. Within her half of the watermill are her weaving loom, spinning wheel, and four different sewing machines. She is a warm and friendly person who everyone gets along with. Working in such close proximity to Keith ensures that their relationship soon blossoms, and work turns into love.

Donna Lambert – Detective Inspector

(Based on Theresa Meadows)

Detective Inspector Donna Lambert is Chief Inspector Paul Johnson's first D.I. when he takes over from his predecessor Chief Inspector Jack Thompson. She proves to be a loyal, courageous police officer. Although badly injured in her first battle with Atkinson and requiring hospital treatment, she recovers to carry on her work. She shows the first inkling of a possible love interest for the new Chief Inspector...but sadly, it never has the chance to blossom. She has the heart of a lion...and owns a protective nature. It is her strength, protection and courage that lead to her ultimate demise during the second devastation to hit the town, where she is trapped in a collapsing police station after saving many lives. The Chief Inspector finds her, but is too late...her loss makes the new Chief Inspector doubt his entire future with the police force.

Keith Johnson – Carpenter

(Based on Keith Johnson)

Not just any old carpenter, this man can turn his hand to anything relating to historical woodcraft. He has a working knowledge of medieval tools, and does not require power to fashion intricate things, such as the components of a weaving loom. His experience proves invaluable to Jamie Winters when it comes to the construction of the water and windmills. Keith is responsible for making all the furniture for the new log cabins. He works in the watermill alongside his partner Diane Sanders, who runs the weaving room next door. They are an extremely-useful team, proving to be the busiest people within the New World commune. Keith was one of the original fifty saved within the shelter in Leeds. Although he prefers to use 15th century tools, his apprenticeship was a modern one in the 21st century. A man of many talents...a true craftsman in every sense of the word, and a hard worker is how this man is known.

Jamie Winters

(Based on Mark Burdette)

Jamie Winters is the brother of Alice Winters-Chambers, and is a very influential man in the New World...although he had to be sent into the past to learn his new role. He is a History graduate whose main influence was the Industrial Revolution. While working on his preserved railway which he purchased with a small loan from his father, logistics mogul Alfred Winters, he was sent back in time with his sister through a strange vortex. That vortex exchanged him and his sister with two Victorian siblings in the first prequel to The Reaper Series, A Switch in Time. In the second prequel, A Woman at the Helm, he is returned even further into the past, to learn the intricacies of water and wind power. He has no understanding at the time of why he has to learn these things, as his passion is steam. After the Apocalypse hits the world, the things he has learned in the past soon come to the fore, as he teams up once again with his best friend Freddie Chambers.

Delphinium

(Based on Katie Sanders)

Delphinium hails from the Realm of Nature…she is a Shape-Shifting Fairy, and is sent to help Sophie Neary as her ink-fairy. Although sent by Mother Nature to keep Sophie's pen filled with ink, Sophie takes to her whole-heartedly, requesting her to stay. At this time, Mother Nature changes Delphinium's role to one of a protector, as well as ink-fairy. Everywhere Sophie goes, you can be sure to find Delphinium sitting upon her shoulder. However, in the blink of an eye, she can change into an Amazonian Warrior. Sophie's life is made complete with the addition of Delphinium as a friend, guide, mentor and protector. In her guise as a fairy, she looks nothing like the classics seen in fairy-tale books; she isn't brightly-coloured, and doesn't wear an acorn shell for a hat. She looks regal; her wings are translucent, and the ribs which hold them in place appear more like twigs than the membranes commonly seen in fairy adaptations. She is very strong, but also very understanding…in fact, she was the perfect choice for Sophie.

Amanda Winters

(Based on Tina McVie Archer)

Amanda Winters materialises in Switch in Time, the first prequel to The Reaper Series. Her character also appears in the following two prequels, and Books 5 & 6 of The Reaper Series. When you first meet her, she is like her daughter Alicia, who is a horribly-spoiled young woman...but by the end of the first prequel, you'll see her very differently. Her character grows in stature during the 2nd and 3rd prequels. She is the wife of billionaire logistics mogul Alfred Winters, and is a socialite...mingling with people of her own ilk, and doing very little else. Her daughter Alicia and son Jamie change all of that when they are switched in time with a pair of Victorian siblings. As Doc Brown says, 'You shouldn't mess with the space-time continuum'...but in Amanda's case, her children running around in the 19th century changed her life forever...for the better, and she becomes the loving mother her children have always wanted.

Alfred Winters

(Based on John Meredith)

Alfred Winters is a quiet and unassuming man. At his place of work, he is often seen tending the trucks...or driving one of them. He is loved by all his work colleagues because of his work ethic, and devotion to duty. In fact, the only difference between Alfred and his co-workers is that he is a billionaire transport mogul, owning the largest logistics company in Great Britain. His family life, however, is much different to his work...only one of his immediate family members shows any respect for him, and that is his son, Jamie. Jamie is also the only one who doesn't view his father as a personal bank. When Alfred has enough of being treated badly by his wife and daughter, he wishes that something could be done to help him in his sorrows. As he drifts off to sleep, someone answers his wish...it isn't the long-dead relative that he hoped for, it is a Deity of Nature who is seeking reasons to save Humanity, which heralds the beginning of A Switch In Time. This seems innocent enough at first, but then leads to the Apocalypse. However, ultimately, it turns into Absolution for his brood...and for mankind.

Tom Harper – Pathology Assistant

(Based on Mikey Sykes)

Tom Harper is the hard-working assistant to Gavin Jackson. He is a studious man of high morals. He is also a qualified Pathologist, and protector of the 'strange creature' which lurks in the morgue…yes – the bane of his working life – Slabgirl. Tom first meets Sarah (aka Slabgirl) when she comes to his department on a school work placement. The previous coroner took a fancy to her (in the wrong way), giving her a job when she left school…Tom intervened upon his bosses' lustful intentions, and has looked after her at work ever since. He is most professional in his work ethic, where Slabgirl enjoys blood and gore…they are as different as chalk and cheese, however he still loves her in his strange way. Unlike his old boss, though, he bears no feelings towards women in this way. His wonderful routine of life is turned upside-down when Slabgirl and his new boss fall in love, and around the same time, he finds love himself with a strange accountant who goes by the name of John Smith.

Mike O'Sullivan Pathology Technician

(Based on Michael O'Sullivan)

Mike O'Sullivan is a scientist, and works in the Pathology Department where Gavin Jackson, Tom Harper and Sarah also work. Mike has been friends with Sarah as long as Tom has...whenever she has a spare minute, she loves to chat with Mike and watch him work. Mike is a very patient man, yet has a strong will...he doesn't suffer fools, and is very impressed with his friend Tom's new boyfriend when he knocks out a group of thugs in their favourite pub, The Viaduct. At his job, he is a hard-working, confident scientist who is in total control of everything...in fact, all of Gavin and Tom's work depends upon the skills of Mike when he performs his tests. No-one knows their field of work as he does...and he takes great pride in that. He is the fourth member of the best Pathology team the hospital has ever had...it is a formidable team, as Gavin Jackson, Tom Harper and Mike O'Sullivan are young go-getters utilizing the very-latest technology...and Slabgirl...well, she makes a great cuppa.

Laura Dinsdale

(Based on Laura Dinsdale)

Laura Dinsdale first appears in our story in the 16th century as the girlfriend of a man Jamie Winters replaces for one week. During his time there, Jamie actually falls in love with Laura, and unbeknownst to either, this meeting occurs simply to mark her for future events. That first meeting is in the second prequel to The Reaper Series, 'A Woman at the Helm'. Laura reappears in the third prequel, 'A Date With the Reaper'. In The Reaper Series itself, however, she first appears in book five, 'Atkinson's Apocalypse', and goes on into book six, 'Atkinson's Absolution'. Her character is complex, as she trips through the centuries in different guises...from 16th century strumpet, to Alfred Winters' personal assistant, ending up as Jamie Winters' wife.

Serbateenium Inspiration Muse

(Based on Emma Hewison)

When the Kraken-Mermaid has laid waste to 99.9% of Humanity, she is not doomed to return to slumber...she is gifted eternal life as her mermaid self, and Mother Nature provides her an abode fit for a queen. To build and decorate this seashore dwelling, she sends one of her Inspiration Muses...and Serbateenium is her Muse of choice. 'Teenie', as she is fondly known, inspires Aquallia's friends to have the dwelling ready for when she awakes. There could not have been a better Muse for this job, as it was Serbateenium who inspired Michelangelo to paint the Sistine Chapel's ceiling... and Sir Christopher Wren to design Saint Paul's Cathedral. She is a hard-working Muse, whose ethic is only bettered by Juliantrium. After her success with Aquallia's dwelling, Mother Nature sends her back onto the Plane of Existence, to help the New Age of Humanity begin again.

Mother Nature

(Based on Beverly Gail Bernett)

Mother Nature is by far my favourite character...not only because she is a kick-ass Goddess in the book (which, of course, she is...), but because of the fact that in real life she is my beautiful wife and muse. As I have stated throughout this entire series in my dedications, it is truly down to her why you have reached this page in The Reaper Series...it was Bevie that gave me the belief that I could write these books...she encouraged me all the way. I really would never have published any of my work if it weren't for her. So...what about the character I wanted her to be? As soon as I discovered that the old lady who gave Alicia Winters the all-important 'marker' ring on a canal bank in 1849 was indeed Mother Nature, this character belonged to Bevie. Mother Nature is the most powerful female in existence...she is the Goddess of

Nature itself. She partnered with Atkinson Senior, and Dewhirst, giving birth to Atkinson Junior, Tamara and Sarah. Her truly good side gave a bad person in the 21st century the chance to redeem herself...and in doing so, she showed pity upon Humanity, when she decided to save 700,000 from total extinction. She showed her Warrior self when she stood her ground with Atkinson Senior, removing two children from his genocidal hands. She showed her Goddess status when she ordered the culling of the human race. Finally, she showed compassion, as she guided what was left of Humanity through its first twelve months of a new existence. She is power personified...she is love personified...she is the beginning of all things, and she loves unconditionally all things. Many of the characteristics of Mother Nature in my stories remind me of my Bevie...in particular, her strong mind, her love and compassion, and her tireless efforts to do good things. However, I am pleased to say she wouldn't have the capability of culling the human race.

About the Author

John Paul Bernett

In 2012, J.P. Bernett published Atkinson's Administration, Book 1 of The Reaper Series...this was his first published work, which he had laboured over off and on for quite some time, with no real thoughts of letting anyone read it. It has been well-documented how that book came to be published, and why this entire series is dedicated to his wife and muse, Beverly Bernett. In the five years since that first book was published, Mr. Bernett has increased his personal works to nine books...including this series, two prequels, and one poetry book containing 160 poems, all written between 2012 and 2017. He has appeared at many events to sign his books, and had the pleasure of meeting folks who have read his Reaper Series. Whilst attending any such event, he dresses in a Victorian style, his signature top hat decorated with pen nibs around the band, and a quill at either side. He looks – and is – quite flamboyant whilst at an event, but this is in stark contrast to how he dresses in everyday life. He is a quiet man, and lives a quiet life...a life in which he writes during the mornings, with the rest of the day being spent with his lovely wife Beverly. When out and about in Whitby, J.P. and his wife are always together. He keeps a low profile, and the way he dresses in his – for lack of a better word – 'normal life' ensures he is seldom-recognized as he walks past with his stick, or pushing Bevie in her wheelchair. Although very approachable, answering any question asked of him about his writing, he never desires nor seeks attention. As a promoter for his work...let's just say, he could do better. When the first book was published, he fulfilled a lifelong ambition, and to him, his every writing goal had been achieved. He would, of course, be happy if a publisher someday discovered his work...but will remain equally happy if they do not. He has no 'ego' as such, and is under no illusions about becoming famous; he is happy to write his books, and look after his wife. There is much more to come from this now-prolific writer; he is halfway through the final prequel to The Reaper Series...A Date With the Reaper. The way this entire series has been written, he could return to his family of Ethereal Warriors whenever he so desires. J.P. Bernett has many more stories to tell...and he will tell them in his way...and in his time. His style of writing would be seen by many as old-fashioned...but as he never panders to any of the new styles of 'superfast reading' trends...this is of no concern to him. He says he will keep telling stories the only way he knows how. It is how he enjoys himself, and he sees no reason to change anytime soon. He lives his life by his favourite motto...the one on the last page of every book he has written... 'Be Happy'...and this writer, although having physical and intellectual difficulties, certainly is.

John Paul Bernett

Be Happy

www.ingramcontent.com/pod-product-compliance
Lightning Source LLC
Chambersburg PA
CBHW072052170626
46813CB00004B/1324

* 9 7 8 0 9 9 2 6 1 7 3 5 6 *